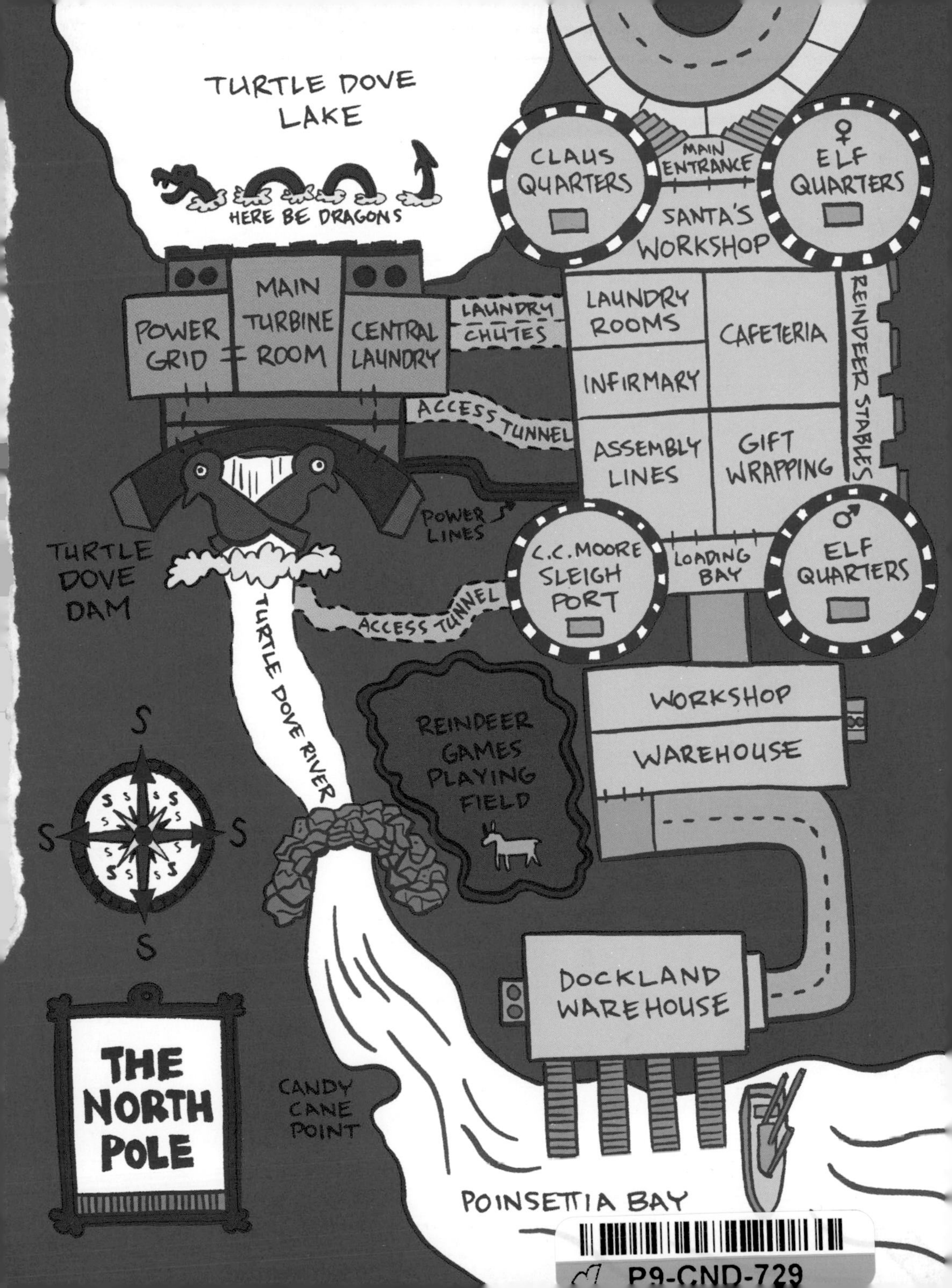
TURTLE DOVE LAKE
HERE BE DRAGONS
CLAUS QUARTERS
MAIN ENTRANCE
ELF QUARTERS
SANTA'S WORKSHOP
POWER GRID
MAIN TURBINE ROOM
CENTRAL LAUNDRY
LAUNDRY CHUTES
LAUNDRY ROOMS
CAFETERIA
INFIRMARY
REINDEER STABLES
ACCESS TUNNEL
ASSEMBLY LINES
GIFT WRAPPING
POWER LINES
TURTLE DOVE DAM
C.C. MOORE SLEIGH PORT
LOADING BAY
ELF QUARTERS
ACCESS TUNNEL
TURTLE DOVE RIVER
WORKSHOP
WAREHOUSE
REINDEER GAMES PLAYING FIELD
S
S
S
S
DOCKLAND WAREHOUSE
THE NORTH POLE
CANDY CANE POINT
POINSETTIA BAY

MANGA CLAUS™

Honor · Loyalty · Tinsel

The Blade of Kringle

By Nathaniel Marunas
Artwork by Erik Craddock

razor
bill

RAZORBILL

PUBLISHED BY THE PENGUIN GROUP

PENGUIN YOUNG READERS GROUP, 345 HUDSON STREET,
NEW YORK, NEW YORK 10014, U.S.A.

PENGUIN GROUP (USA) INC., 375 HUDSON STREET,
NEW YORK, NEW YORK 10014, U.S.A.

PENGUIN GROUP (CANADA), 90 EGLINTON AVENUE EAST,
SUITE 700, TORONTO, ONTARIO, CANADA M4P 2Y3
(A DIVISION OF PEARSON PENGUIN CANADA INC.)

PENGUIN BOOKS LTD, 80 STRAND, LONDON WC2R 0RL, ENGLAND

PENGUIN IRELAND, 25 ST STEPHEN'S GREEN, DUBLIN 2, IRELAND
(A DIVISION OF PENGUIN BOOKS LTD)

PENGUIN GROUP (AUSTRALIA), 250 CAMBERWELL ROAD,
CAMBERWELL, VICTORIA 3124, AUSTRALIA
(A DIVISION OF PEARSON AUSTRALIA GROUP PTY LTD)

PENGUIN BOOKS INDIA PVT LTD, 11 COMMUNITY CENTRE,
PANCHSHEEL PARK, NEW DELHI – 110 017, INDIA

PENGUIN GROUP (NZ), CNR AIRBORNE AND ROSEDALE ROADS,
ALBANY, AUCKLAND 1310, NEW ZEALAND
(A DIVISION OF PEARSON NEW ZEALAND LTD)

PENGUIN BOOKS (SOUTH AFRICA) (PTY) LTD,
24 STURDEE AVENUE, ROSEBANK, JOHANNESBURG 2196,
SOUTH AFRICA

PENGUIN BOOKS LTD, REGISTERED OFFICES:
80 STRAND, LONDON WC2R 0RL, ENGLAND

A QUIRK PACKAGING BOOK

10 9 8 7 6 5 4 3 2 1

COPYRIGHT 2006 © QUIRK PACKAGING, INC.

TEXT COPYRIGHT 2006 © NATHANIEL MARUNAS
ILLUSTRATIONS COPYRIGHT 2006 © ERIK CRADDOCK
COLORING BY ERIK CRADDOCK, MARION VITUS, AND JOHN GREEN
LETTERING BY MARION VITUS

ALL RIGHTS RESERVED

LIBRARY OF CONGRESS CATALOGING-IN-PUBLICATION DATA
IS AVAILABLE

MANUFACTURED IN CHINA

THE SCANNING, UPLOADING AND DISTRIBUTION OF THIS BOOK
VIA THE INTERNET OR VIA ANY OTHER MEANS WITHOUT THE
PERMISSION OF THE PUBLISHER IS ILLEGAL AND PUNISHABLE
BY LAW. PLEASE PURCHASE ONLY AUTHORIZED ELECTRONIC
EDITIONS, AND DO NOT PARTICIPATE IN OR ENCOURAGE
ELECTRONIC PIRACY OF COPYRIGHTED MATERIALS. YOUR
SUPPORT OF THE AUTHOR'S RIGHTS IS APPRECIATED.

THE PUBLISHER DOES NOT HAVE ANY CONTROL OVER AND
DOES NOT ASSUME ANY RESPONSIBILITY FOR AUTHOR OR
THIRD-PARTY WEBSITES OR THEIR CONTENT.

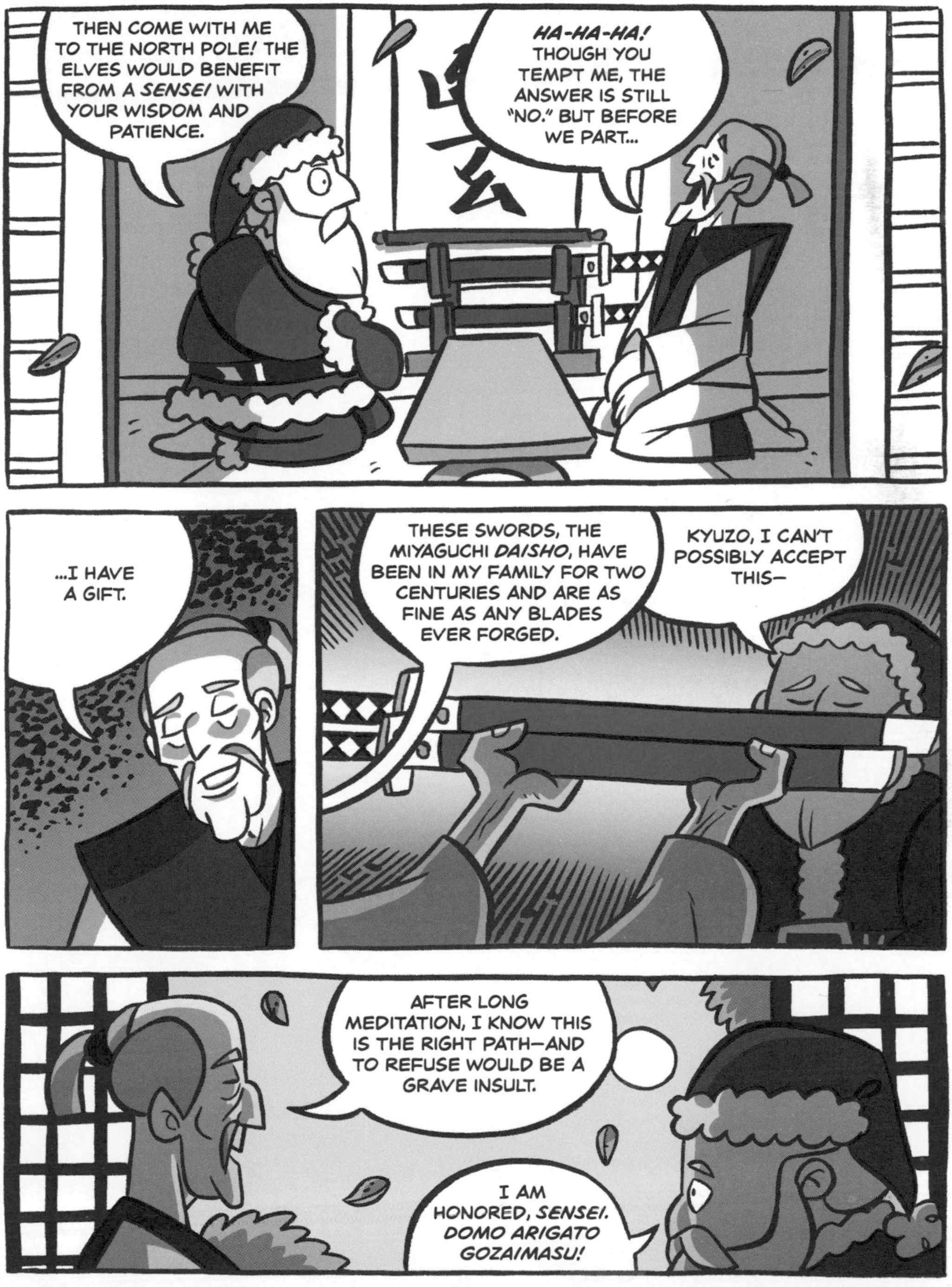
THEN COME WITH ME TO THE NORTH POLE! THE ELVES WOULD BENEFIT FROM A *SENSEI* WITH YOUR WISDOM AND PATIENCE.
HA-HA-HA! THOUGH YOU TEMPT ME, THE ANSWER IS STILL "NO." BUT BEFORE WE PART...
...I HAVE A GIFT.
THESE SWORDS, THE MIYAGUCHI *DAISHO*, HAVE BEEN IN MY FAMILY FOR TWO CENTURIES AND ARE AS FINE AS ANY BLADES EVER FORGED.
KYUZO, I CAN'T POSSIBLY ACCEPT THIS—
AFTER LONG MEDITATION, I KNOW THIS IS THE RIGHT PATH—AND TO REFUSE WOULD BE A GRAVE INSULT.
I AM HONORED, *SENSEI*. *DOMO ARIGATO GOZAIMASU!*

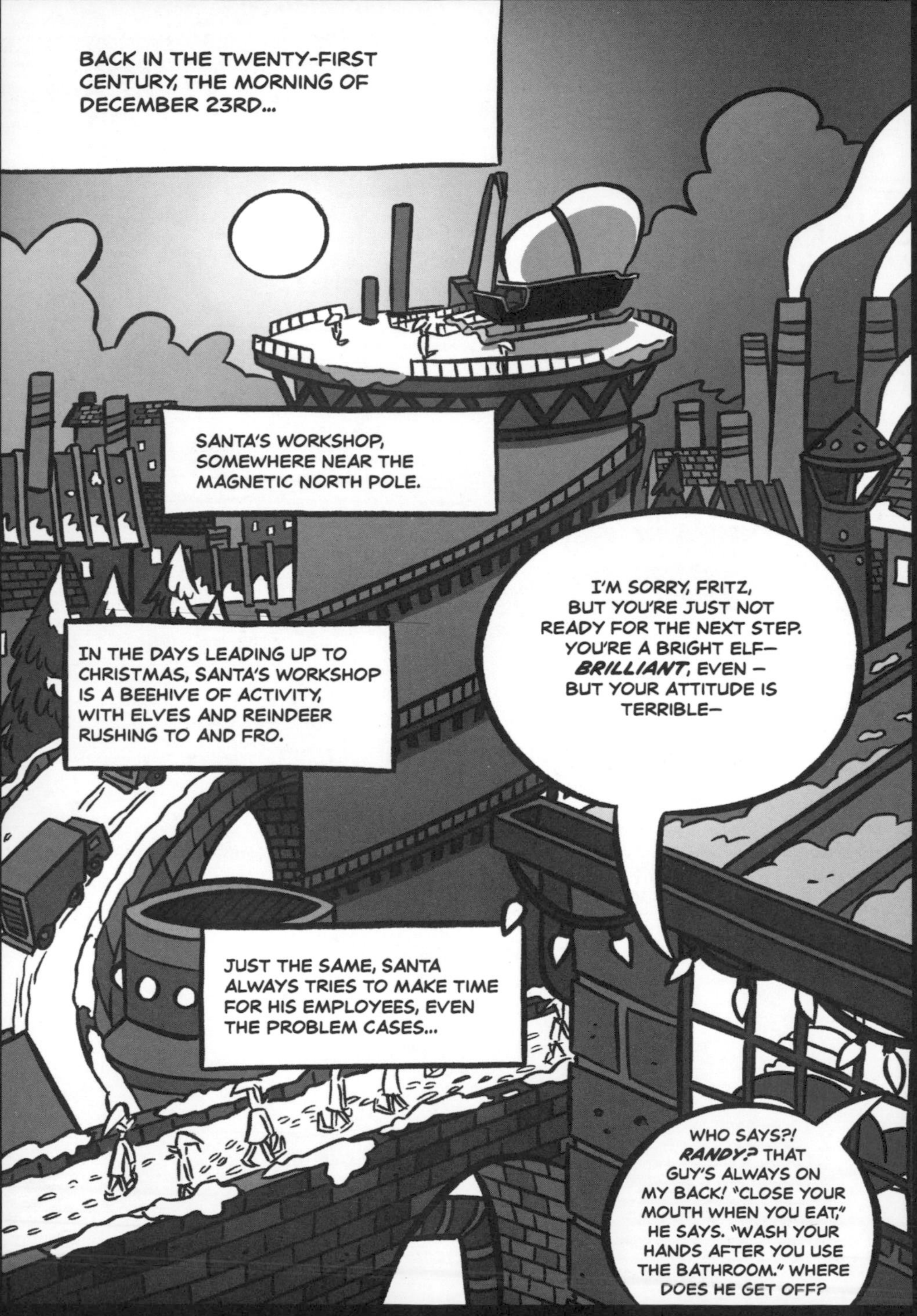
BACK IN THE TWENTY-FIRST CENTURY, THE MORNING OF DECEMBER 23RD...
SANTA'S WORKSHOP, SOMEWHERE NEAR THE MAGNETIC NORTH POLE.
IN THE DAYS LEADING UP TO CHRISTMAS, SANTA'S WORKSHOP IS A BEEHIVE OF ACTIVITY, WITH ELVES AND REINDEER RUSHING TO AND FRO.
I'M SORRY, FRITZ, BUT YOU'RE JUST NOT READY FOR THE NEXT STEP. YOU'RE A BRIGHT ELF— *BRILLIANT*, EVEN — BUT YOUR ATTITUDE IS TERRIBLE—
JUST THE SAME, SANTA ALWAYS TRIES TO MAKE TIME FOR HIS EMPLOYEES, EVEN THE PROBLEM CASES...
WHO SAYS?! *RANDY?* THAT GUY'S ALWAYS ON MY BACK! "CLOSE YOUR MOUTH WHEN YOU EAT," HE SAYS. "WASH YOUR HANDS AFTER YOU USE THE BATHROOM." WHERE DOES HE GET OFF?

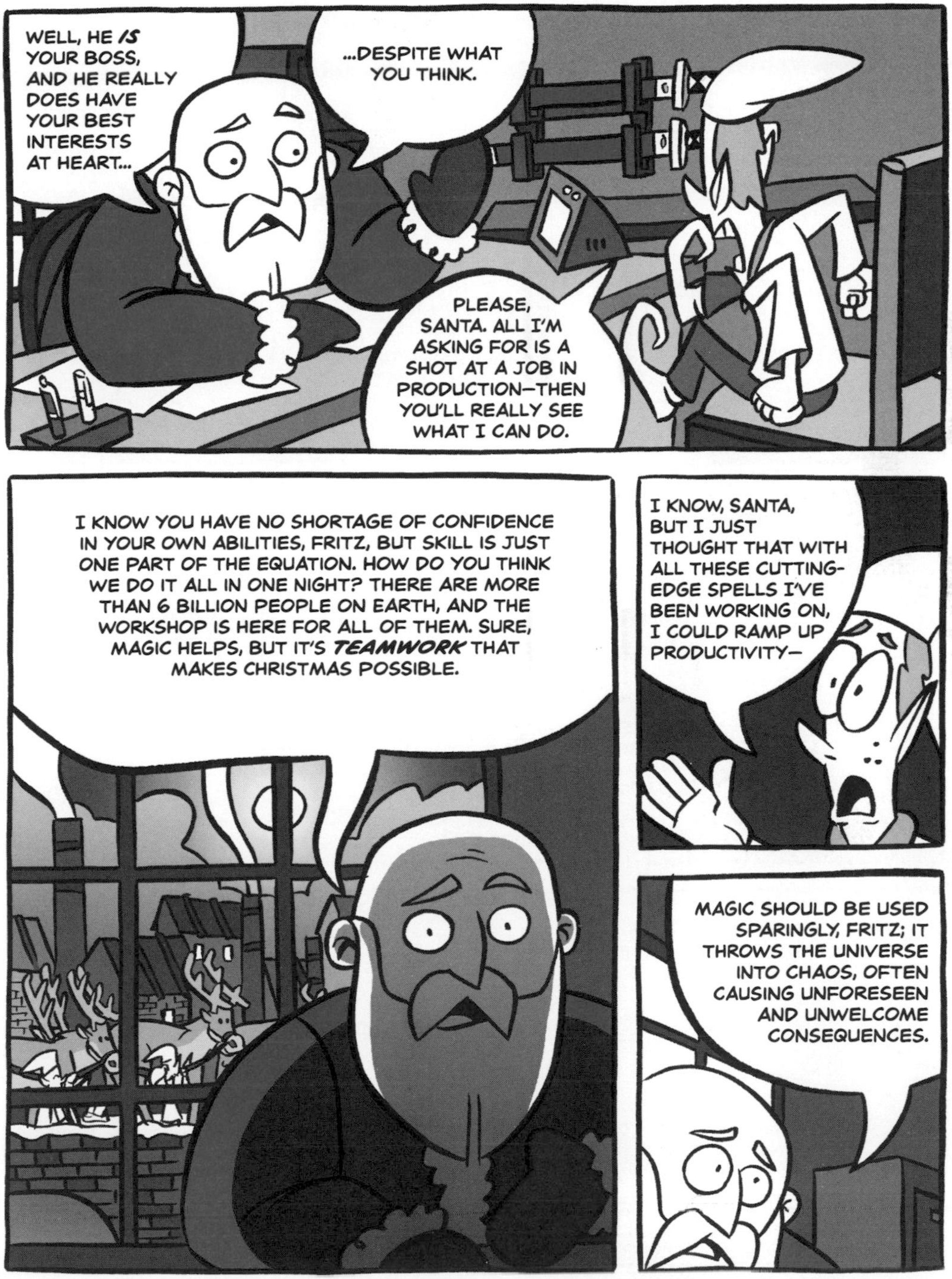
WELL, HE *IS* YOUR BOSS, AND HE REALLY DOES HAVE YOUR BEST INTERESTS AT HEART...
...DESPITE WHAT YOU THINK.
PLEASE, SANTA. ALL I'M ASKING FOR IS A SHOT AT A JOB IN PRODUCTION—THEN YOU'LL REALLY SEE WHAT I CAN DO.
I KNOW YOU HAVE NO SHORTAGE OF CONFIDENCE IN YOUR OWN ABILITIES, FRITZ, BUT SKILL IS JUST ONE PART OF THE EQUATION. HOW DO YOU THINK WE DO IT ALL IN ONE NIGHT? THERE ARE MORE THAN 6 BILLION PEOPLE ON EARTH, AND THE WORKSHOP IS HERE FOR ALL OF THEM. SURE, MAGIC HELPS, BUT IT'S ***TEAMWORK*** THAT MAKES CHRISTMAS POSSIBLE.
I KNOW, SANTA, BUT I JUST THOUGHT THAT WITH ALL THESE CUTTING-EDGE SPELLS I'VE BEEN WORKING ON, I COULD RAMP UP PRODUCTIVITY—
MAGIC SHOULD BE USED SPARINGLY, FRITZ; IT THROWS THE UNIVERSE INTO CHAOS, OFTEN CAUSING UNFORESEEN AND UNWELCOME CONSEQUENCES.

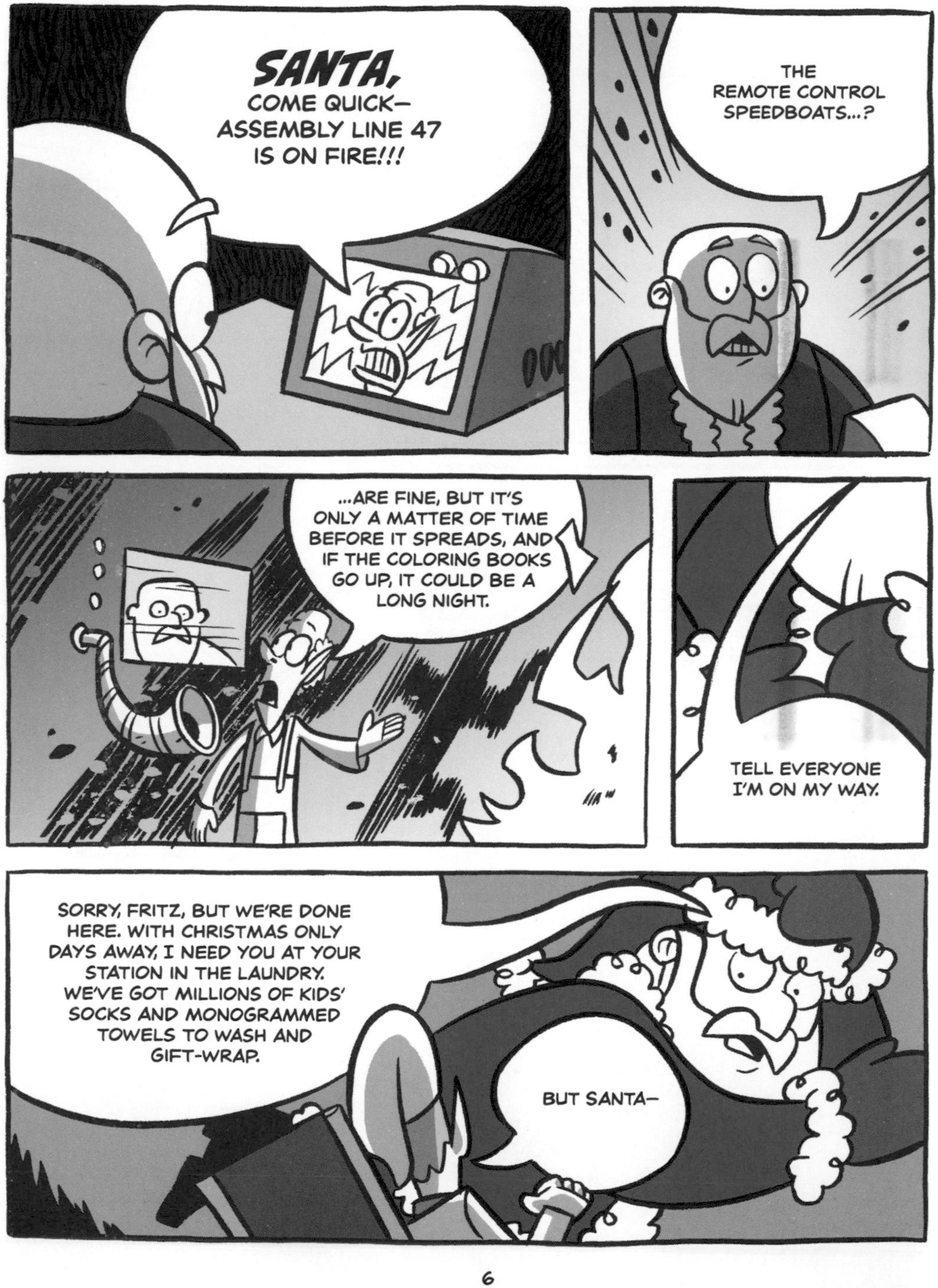
SANTA, COME QUICK— ASSEMBLY LINE 47 IS ON FIRE!!!
THE REMOTE CONTROL SPEEDBOATS...?
...ARE FINE, BUT IT'S ONLY A MATTER OF TIME BEFORE IT SPREADS, AND IF THE COLORING BOOKS GO UP, IT COULD BE A LONG NIGHT.
TELL EVERYONE I'M ON MY WAY.
SORRY, FRITZ, BUT WE'RE DONE HERE. WITH CHRISTMAS ONLY DAYS AWAY, I NEED YOU AT YOUR STATION IN THE LAUNDRY. WE'VE GOT MILLIONS OF KIDS' SOCKS AND MONOGRAMMED TOWELS TO WASH AND GIFT-WRAP.
BUT SANTA—

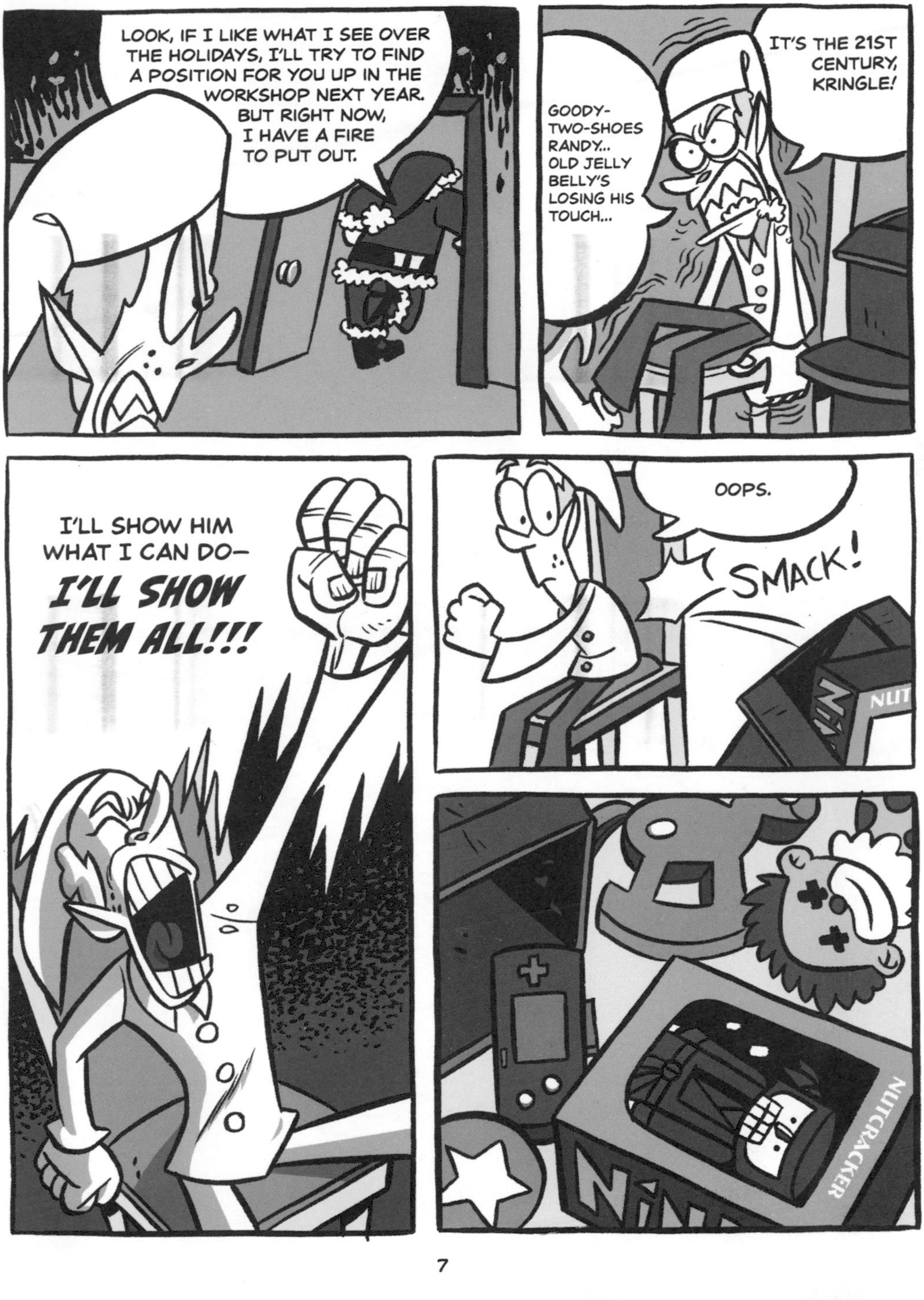
LOOK, IF I LIKE WHAT I SEE OVER THE HOLIDAYS, I'LL TRY TO FIND A POSITION FOR YOU UP IN THE WORKSHOP NEXT YEAR. BUT RIGHT NOW, I HAVE A FIRE TO PUT OUT.
IT'S THE 21ST CENTURY, KRINGLE!
GOODY-TWO-SHOES RANDY... OLD JELLY BELLY'S LOSING HIS TOUCH...
I'LL SHOW HIM WHAT I CAN DO—
I'LL SHOW THEM ALL!!!
OOPS.
SMACK!
NUTCRACKER

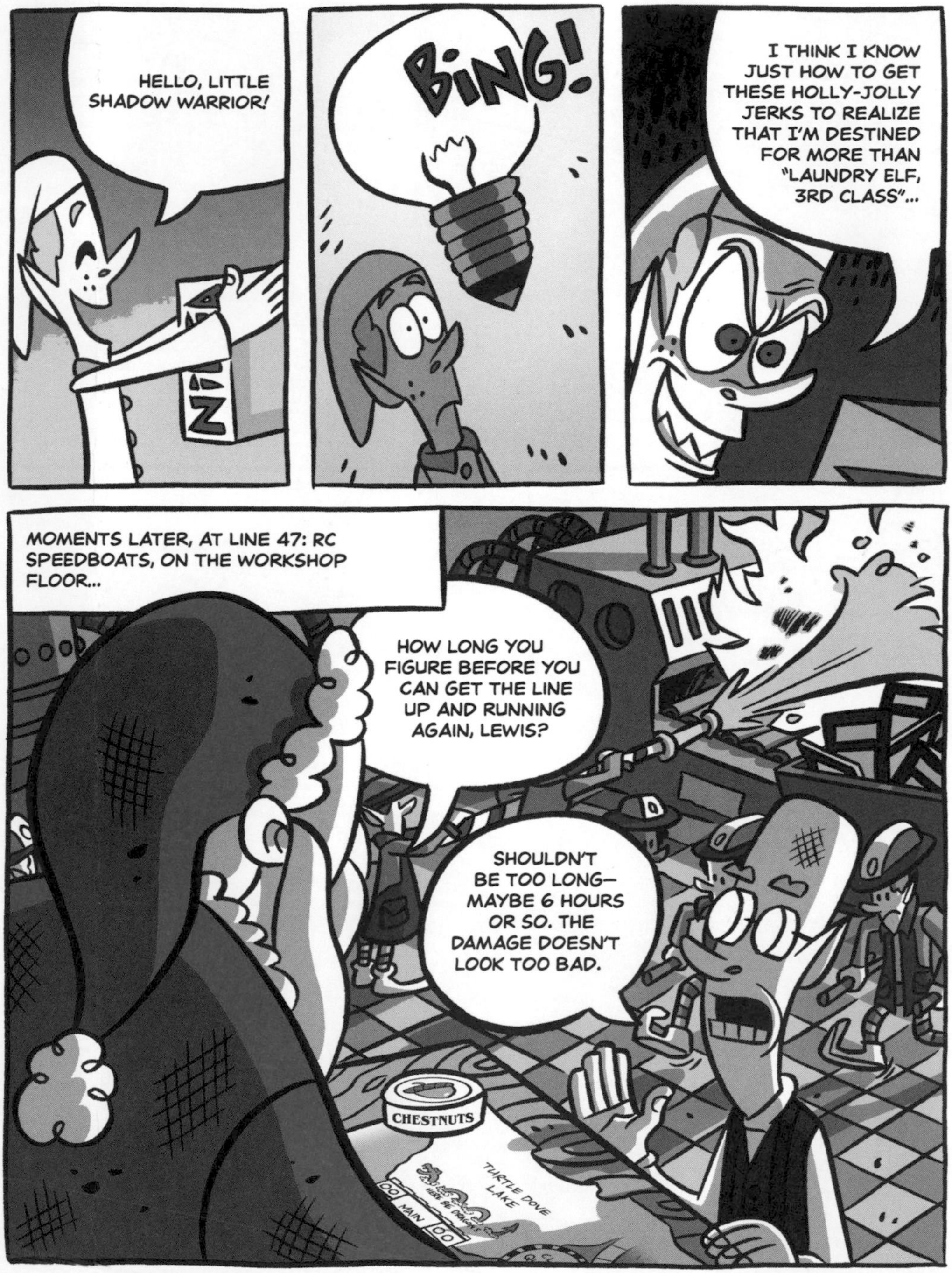
HELLO, LITTLE SHADOW WARRIOR!
BING!
I THINK I KNOW JUST HOW TO GET THESE HOLLY-JOLLY JERKS TO REALIZE THAT I'M DESTINED FOR MORE THAN "LAUNDRY ELF, 3RD CLASS"...
MOMENTS LATER, AT LINE 47: RC SPEEDBOATS, ON THE WORKSHOP FLOOR...
HOW LONG YOU FIGURE BEFORE YOU CAN GET THE LINE UP AND RUNNING AGAIN, LEWIS?
SHOULDN'T BE TOO LONG—MAYBE 6 HOURS OR SO. THE DAMAGE DOESN'T LOOK TOO BAD.
CHESTNUTS
TURTLE DOVE LAKE
MAIN

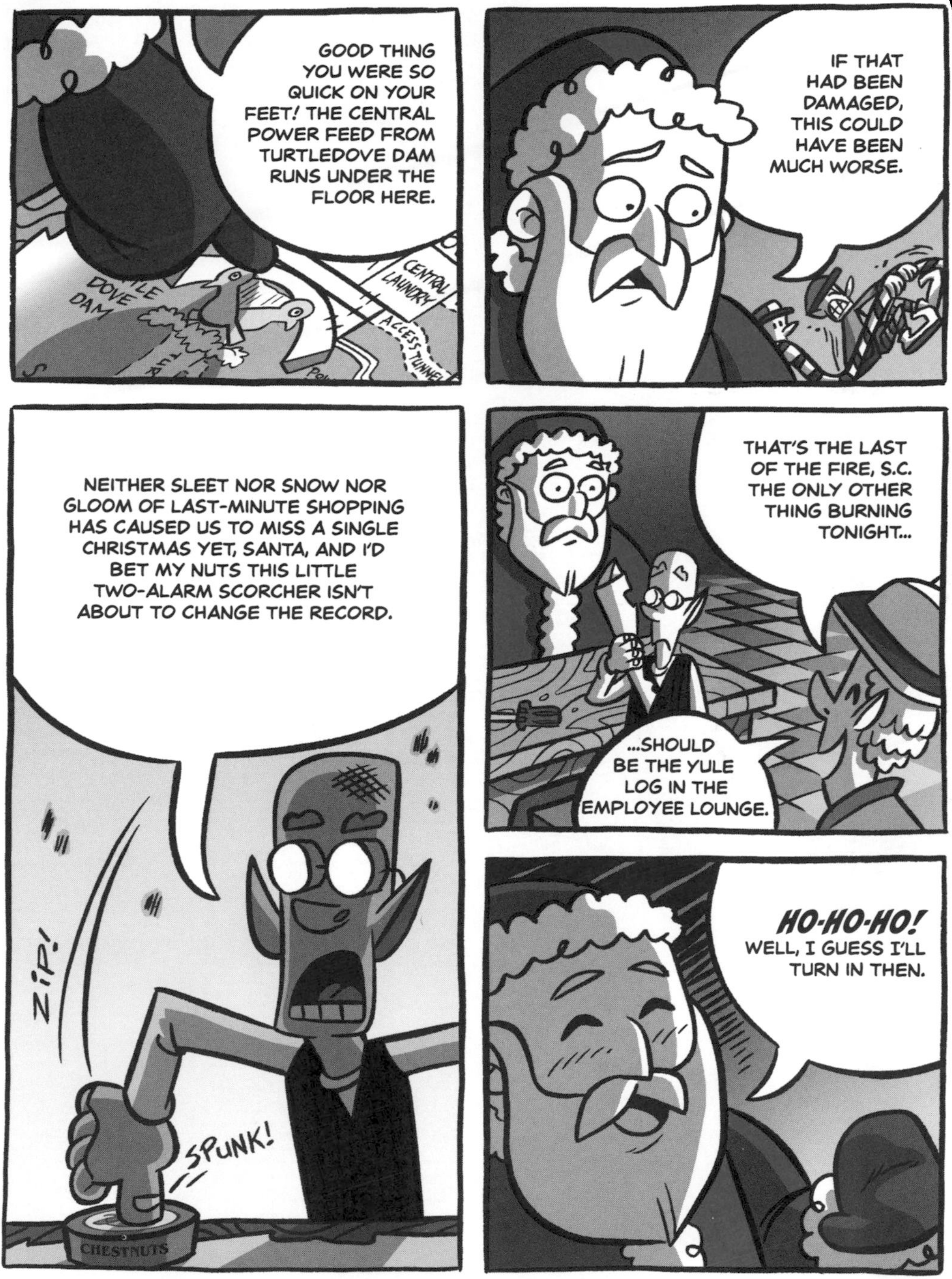
GOOD THING YOU WERE SO QUICK ON YOUR FEET! THE CENTRAL POWER FEED FROM TURTLEDOVE DAM RUNS UNDER THE FLOOR HERE.
CENTRAL LAUNDRY
ACCESS TUNNEL
DOVE DAM
IF THAT HAD BEEN DAMAGED, THIS COULD HAVE BEEN MUCH WORSE.
NEITHER SLEET NOR SNOW NOR GLOOM OF LAST-MINUTE SHOPPING HAS CAUSED US TO MISS A SINGLE CHRISTMAS YET, SANTA, AND I'D BET MY NUTS THIS LITTLE TWO-ALARM SCORCHER ISN'T ABOUT TO CHANGE THE RECORD.
ZIP!
SPUNK!
CHESTNUTS
THAT'S THE LAST OF THE FIRE, S.C. THE ONLY OTHER THING BURNING TONIGHT...
...SHOULD BE THE YULE LOG IN THE EMPLOYEE LOUNGE.
HO-HO-HO! WELL, I GUESS I'LL TURN IN THEN.

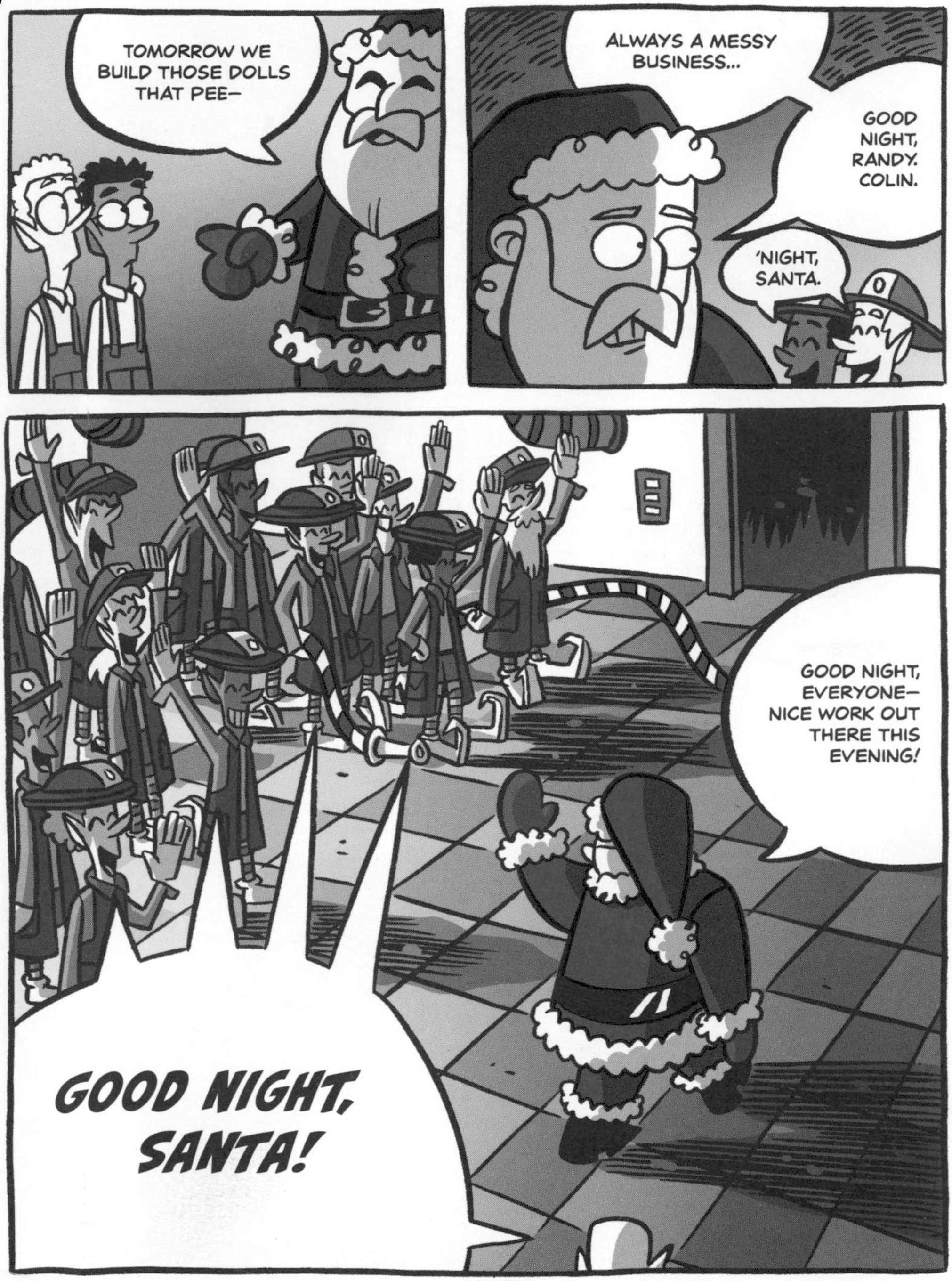
TOMORROW WE BUILD THOSE DOLLS THAT PEE—
ALWAYS A MESSY BUSINESS...
GOOD NIGHT, RANDY. COLIN.
'NIGHT, SANTA.
GOOD NIGHT, EVERYONE— NICE WORK OUT THERE THIS EVENING!
GOOD NIGHT, SANTA!

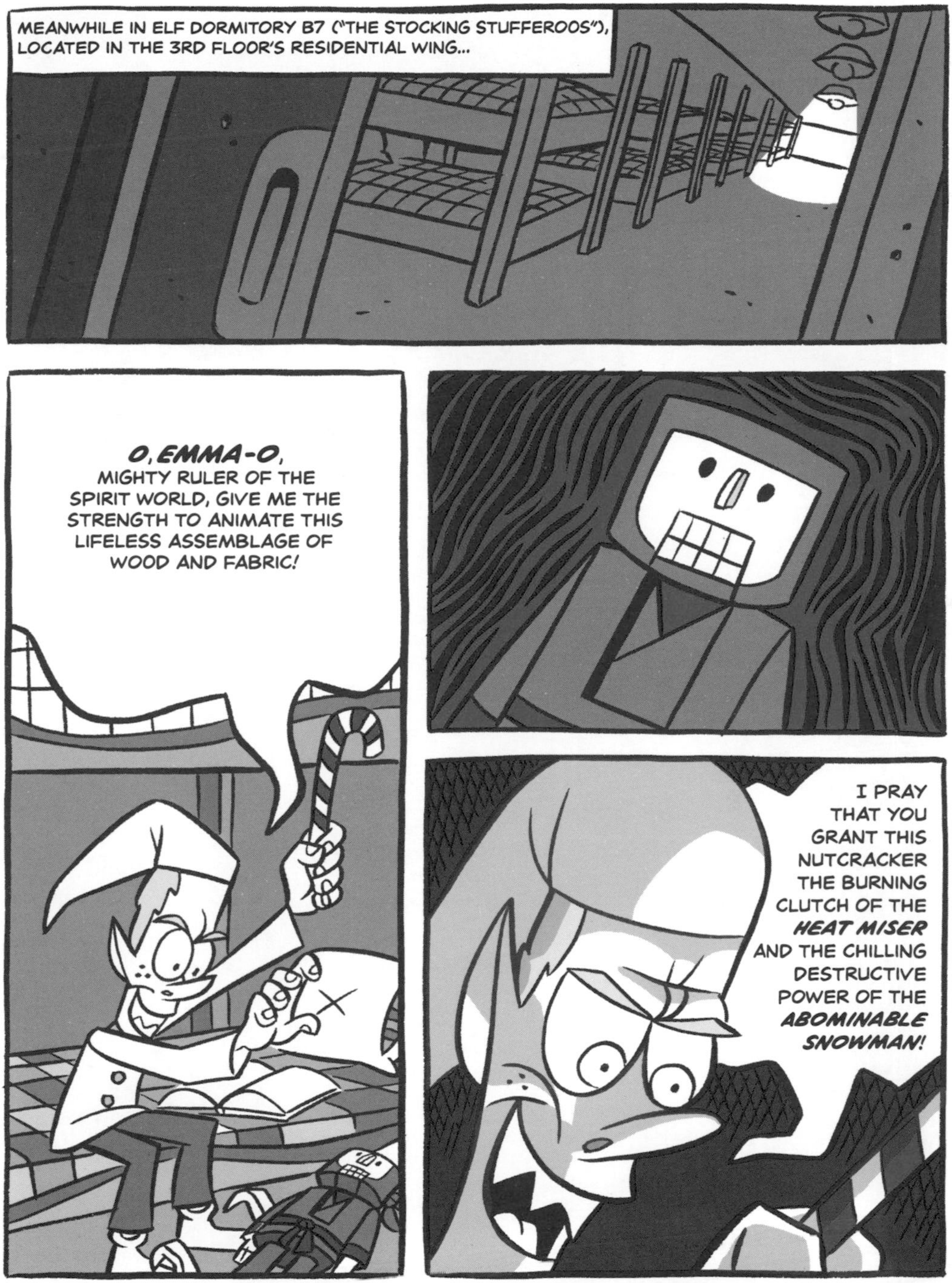
MEANWHILE IN ELF DORMITORY B7 ("THE STOCKING STUFFEROOS"), LOCATED IN THE 3RD FLOOR'S RESIDENTIAL WING...
O, EMMA-O, MIGHTY RULER OF THE SPIRIT WORLD, GIVE ME THE STRENGTH TO ANIMATE THIS LIFELESS ASSEMBLAGE OF WOOD AND FABRIC!
I PRAY THAT YOU GRANT THIS NUTCRACKER THE BURNING CLUTCH OF THE HEAT MISER AND THE CHILLING DESTRUCTIVE POWER OF THE ABOMINABLE SNOWMAN!

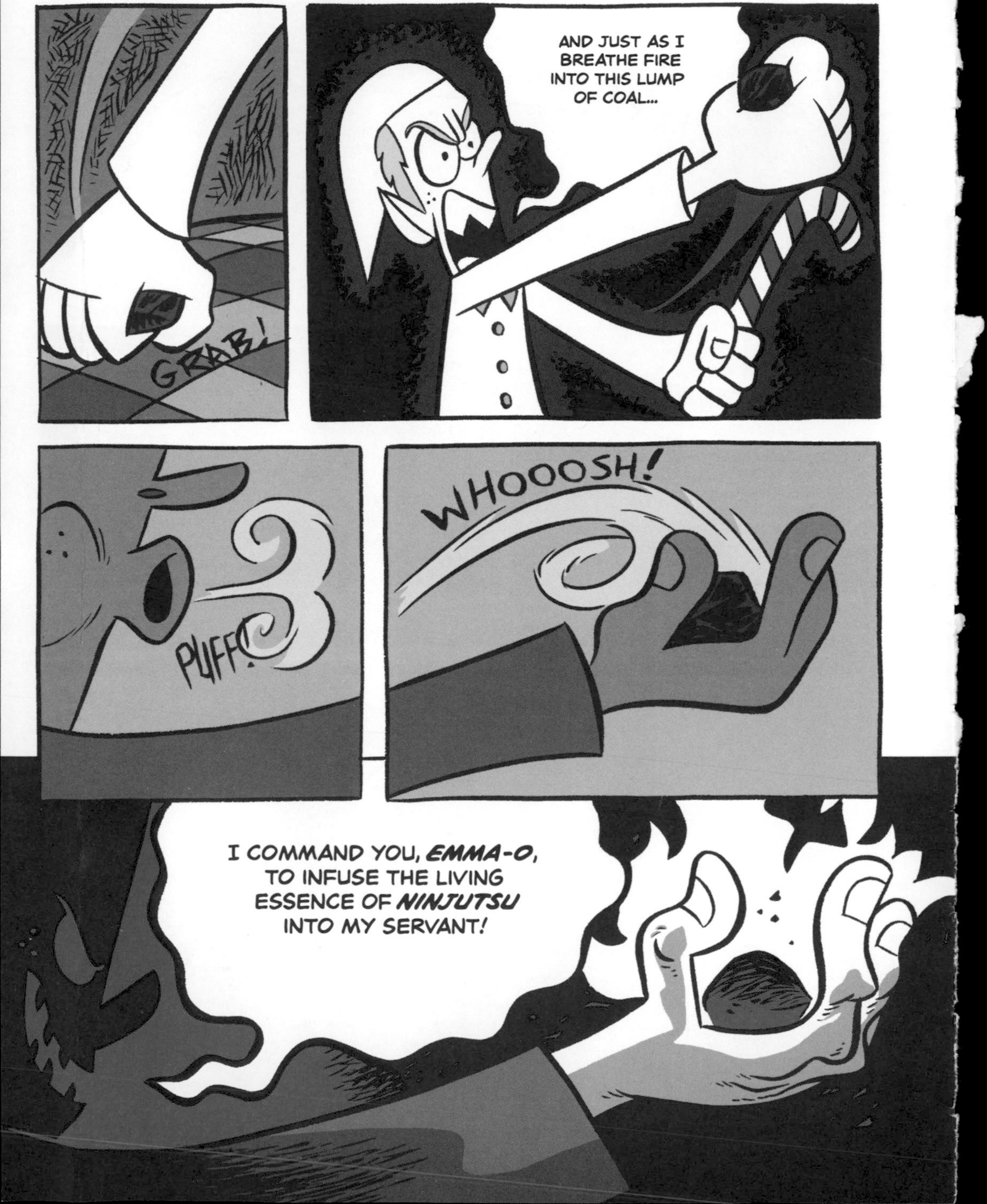
GRAB!
AND JUST AS I BREATHE FIRE INTO THIS LUMP OF COAL...
PUFF!
WHOOOSH!
I COMMAND YOU, *EMMA-O*, TO INFUSE THE LIVING ESSENCE OF *NINJUTSU* INTO MY SERVANT!

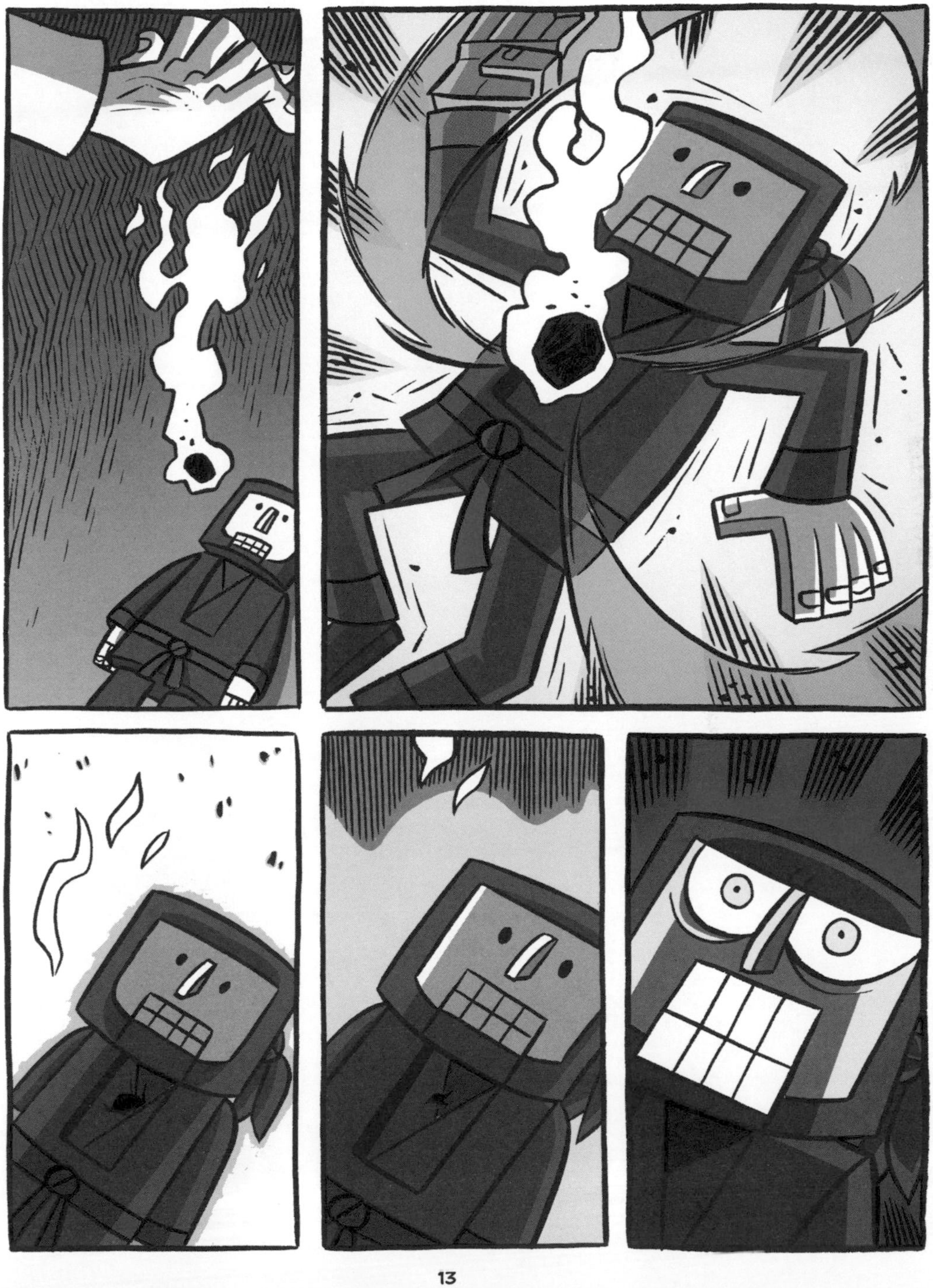

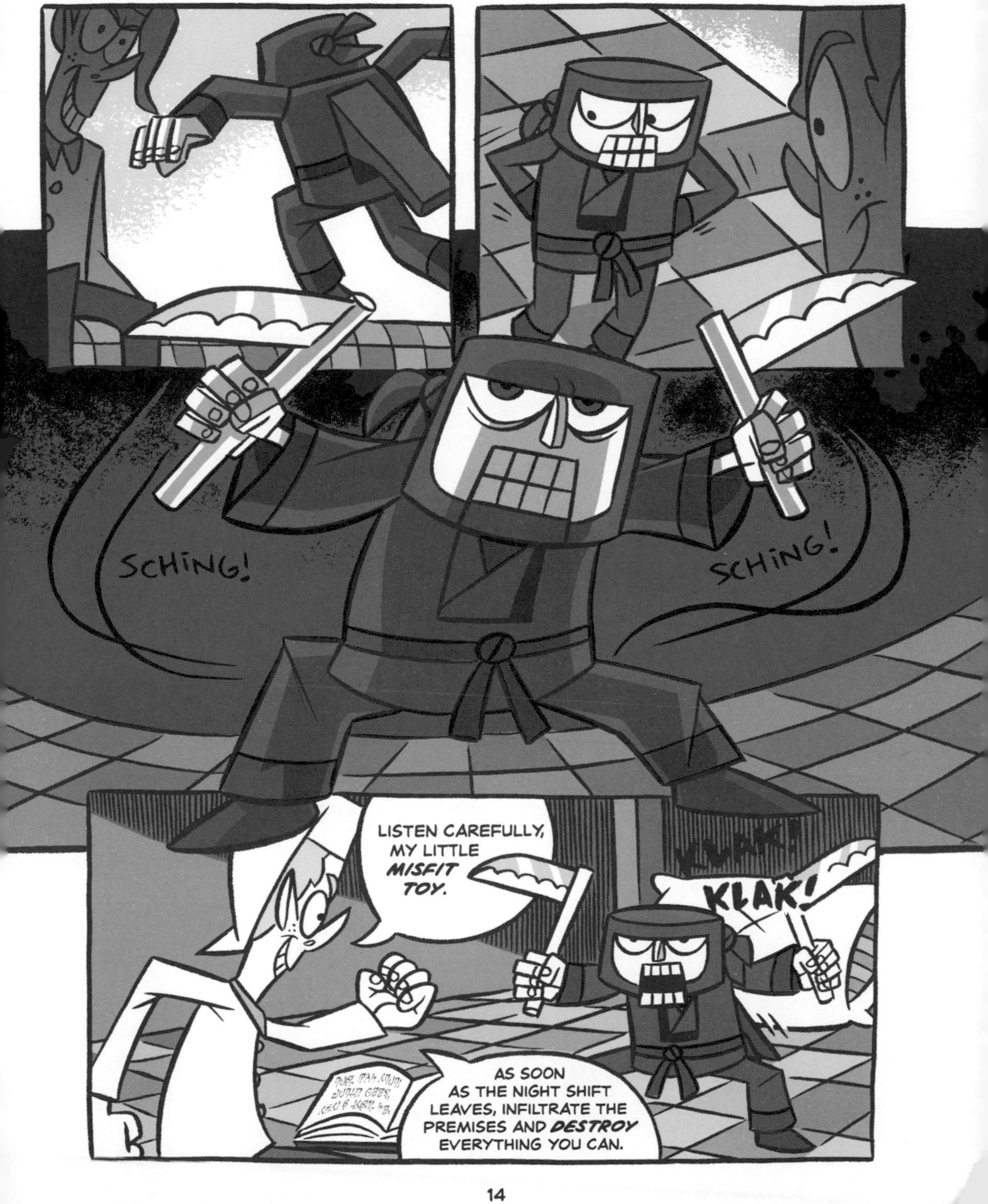

SCHING!
SCHING!
LISTEN CAREFULLY, MY LITTLE *MISFIT TOY.*
KLAK!
KLAK!
AS SOON AS THE NIGHT SHIFT LEAVES, INFILTRATE THE PREMISES AND *DESTROY* EVERYTHING YOU CAN.

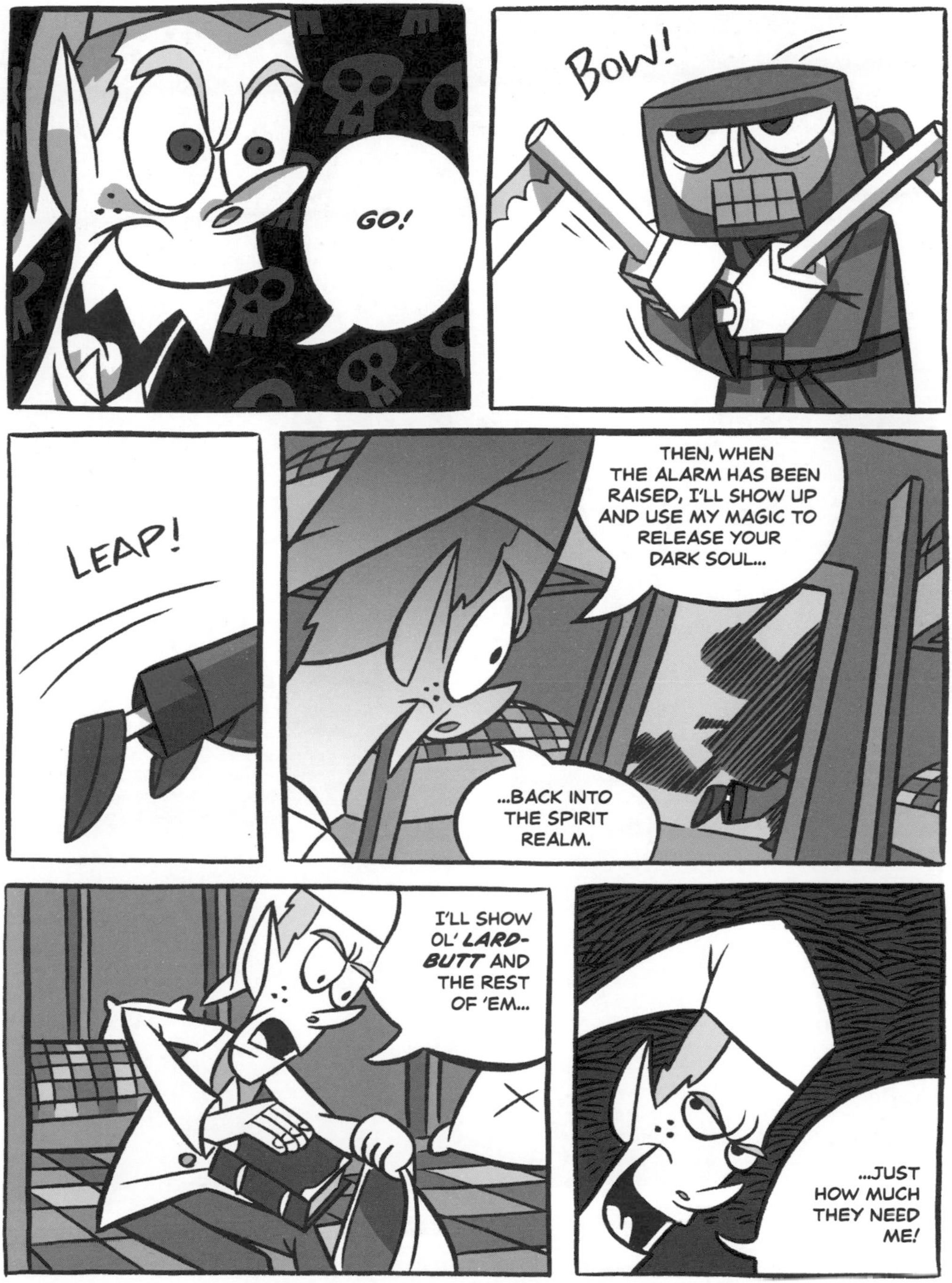
GO!
BOW!
LEAP!
THEN, WHEN THE ALARM HAS BEEN RAISED, I'LL SHOW UP AND USE MY MAGIC TO RELEASE YOUR DARK SOUL...
...BACK INTO THE SPIRIT REALM.
I'LL SHOW OL' LARD-BUTT AND THE REST OF 'EM...
...JUST HOW MUCH THEY NEED ME!

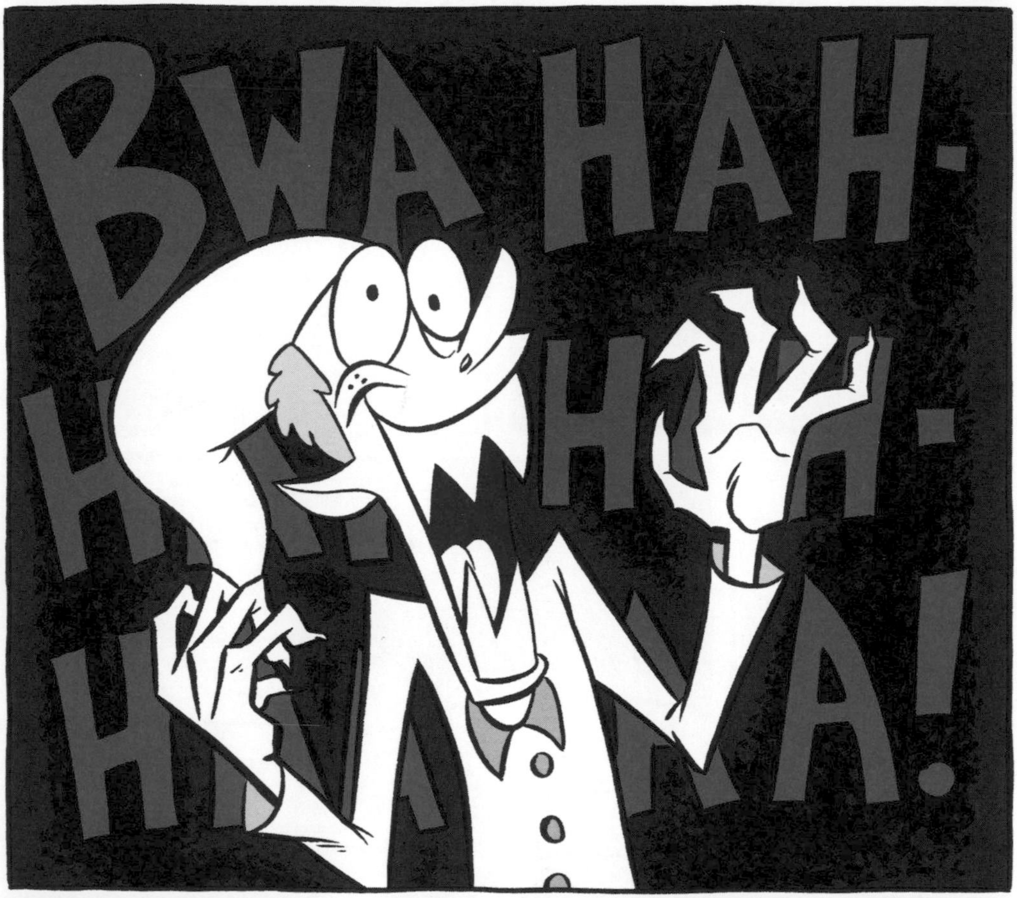
BWA HAH-HAH-HAH-HAH-HA!

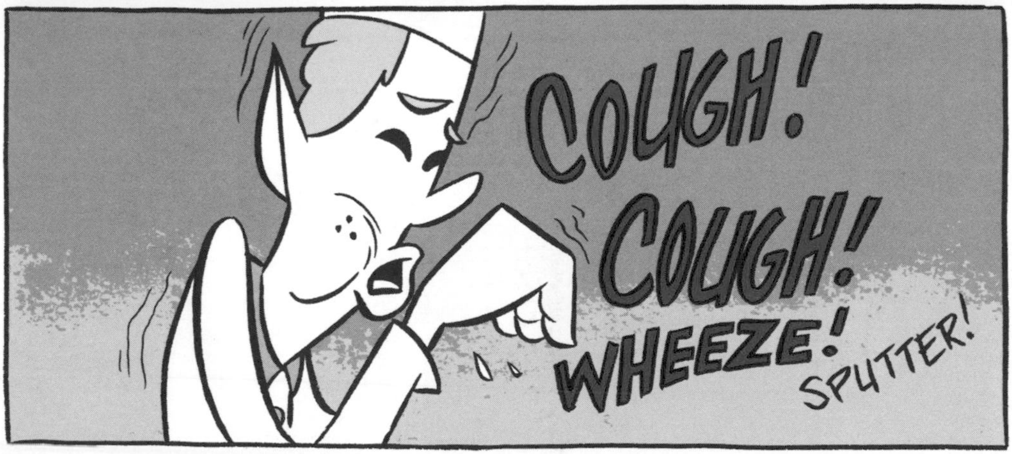
COUGH!
COUGH!
WHEEZE!
SPUTTER!

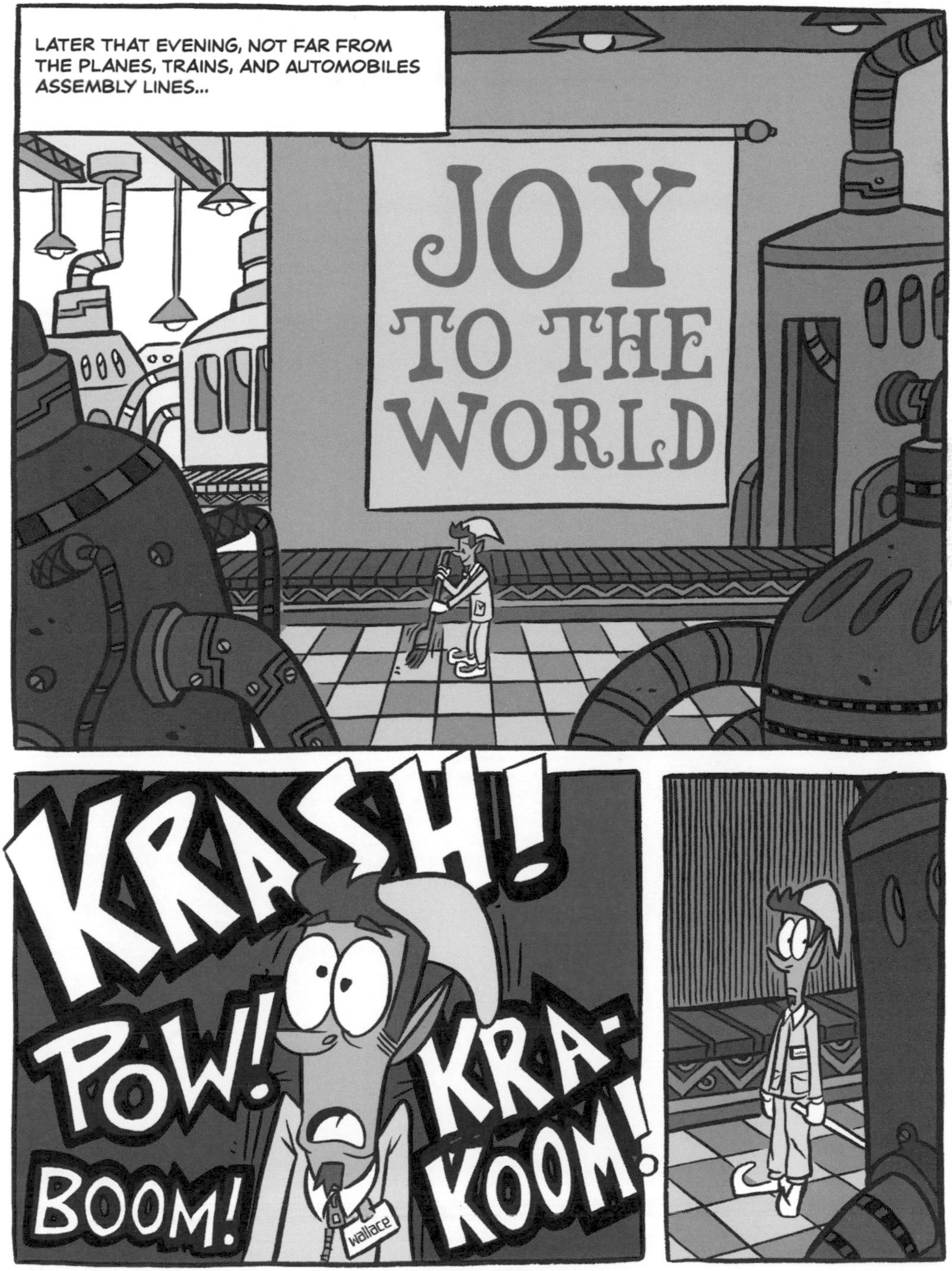
LATER THAT EVENING, NOT FAR FROM THE PLANES, TRAINS, AND AUTOMOBILES ASSEMBLY LINES...
JOY TO THE WORLD
KRASH!
POW!
BOOM!
KRA-KOOM!
wallace

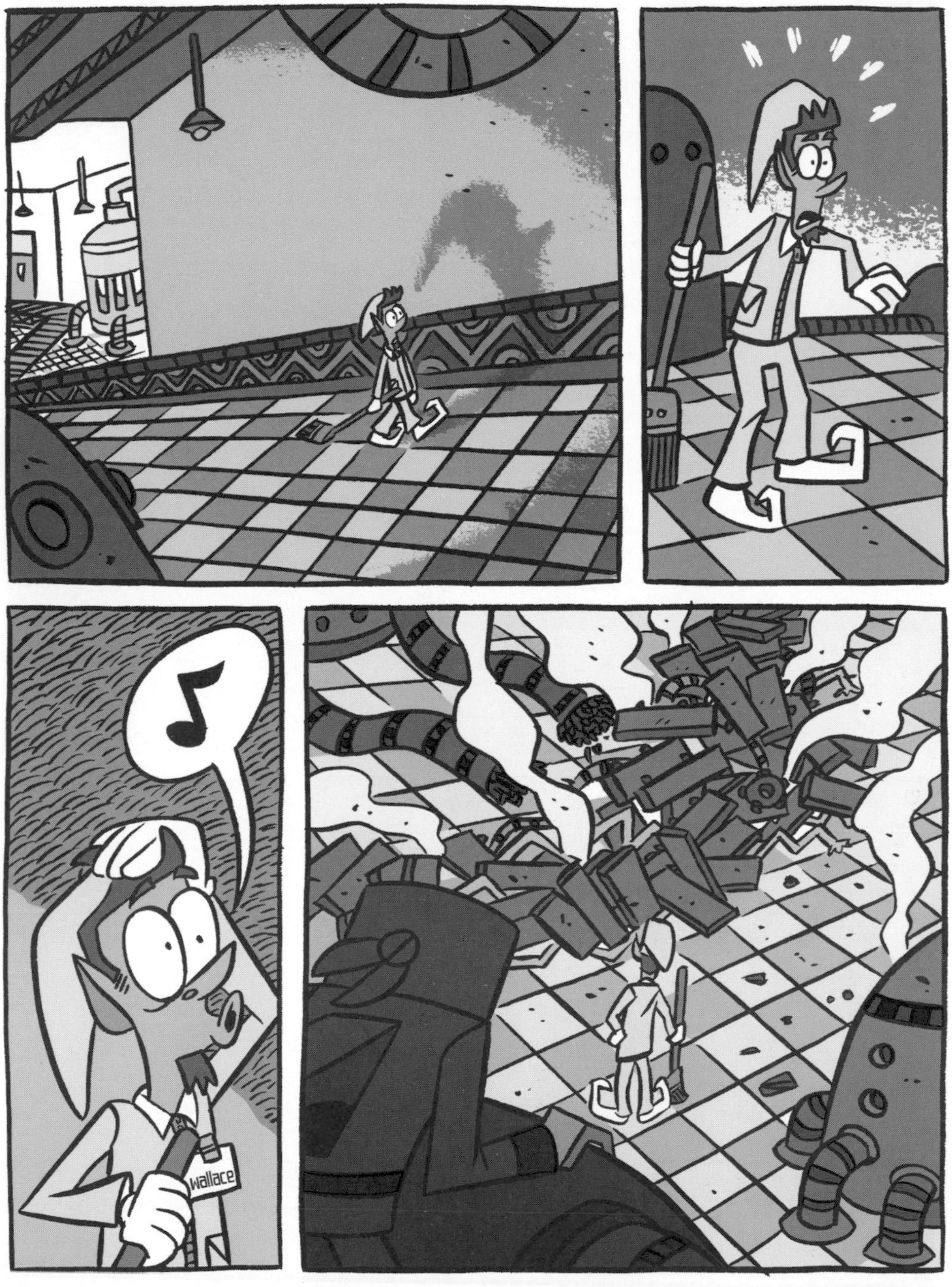
wallace

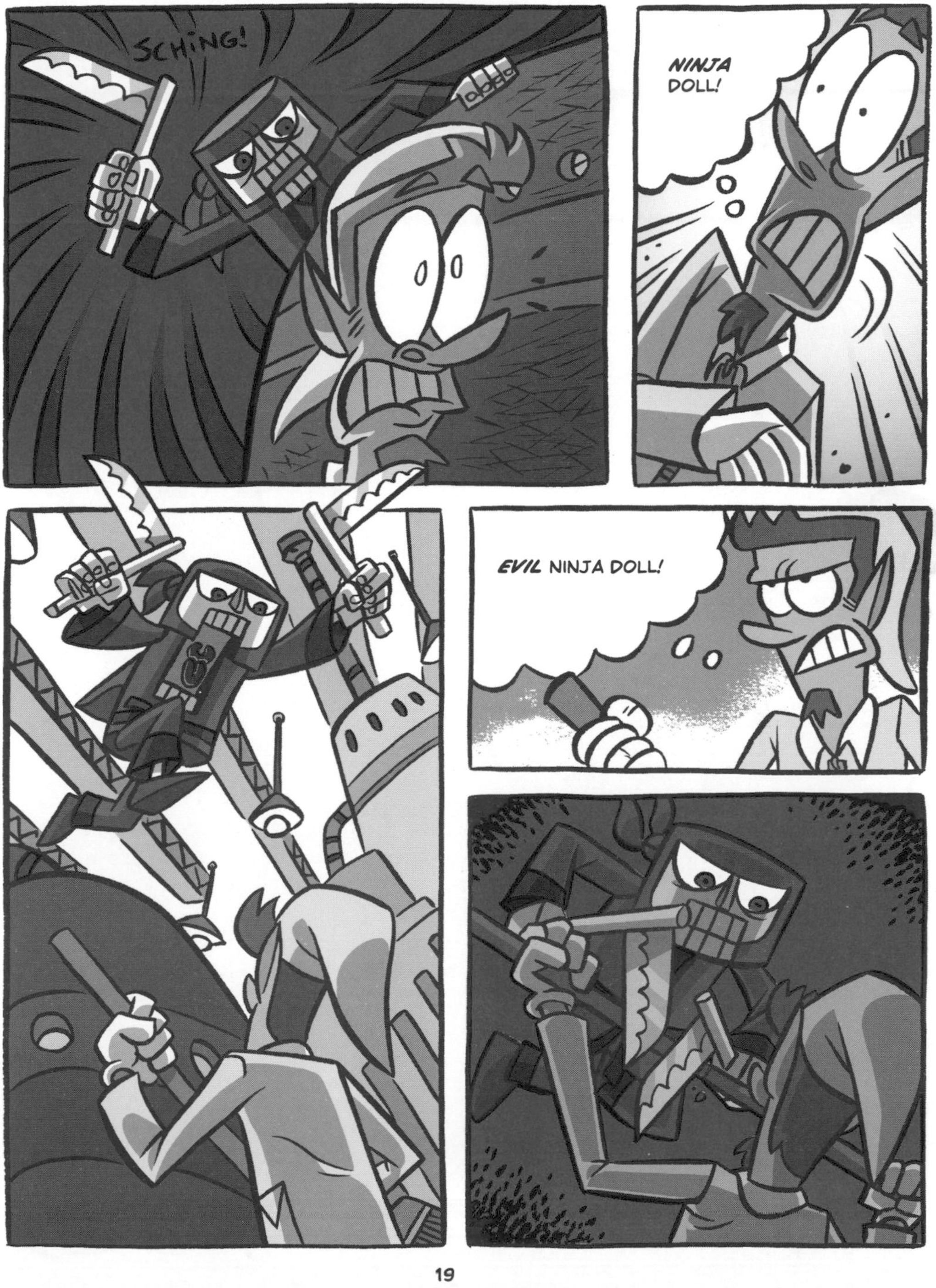
SCHING!
NINJA DOLL!
EVIL NINJA DOLL!

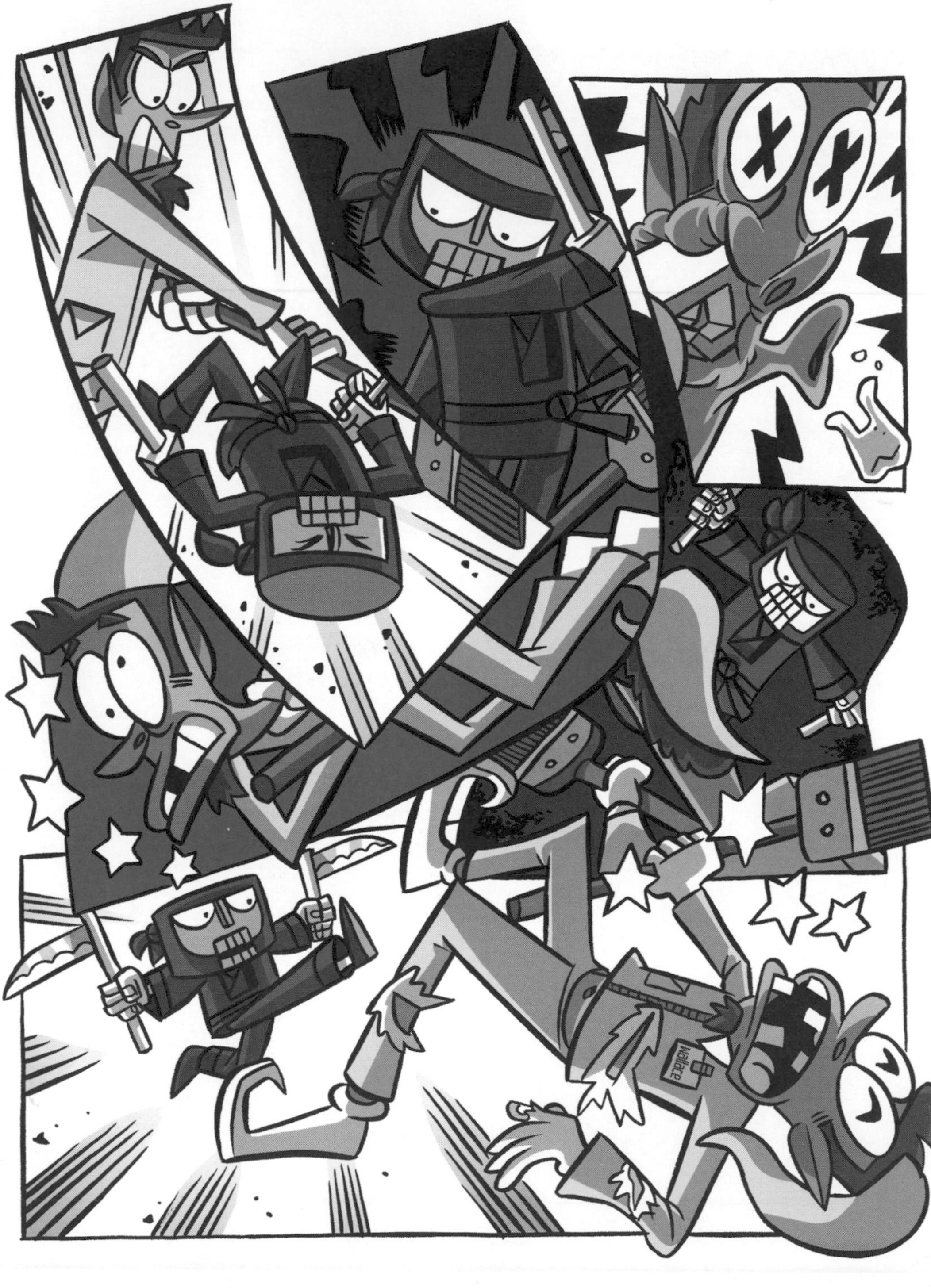
Wallace

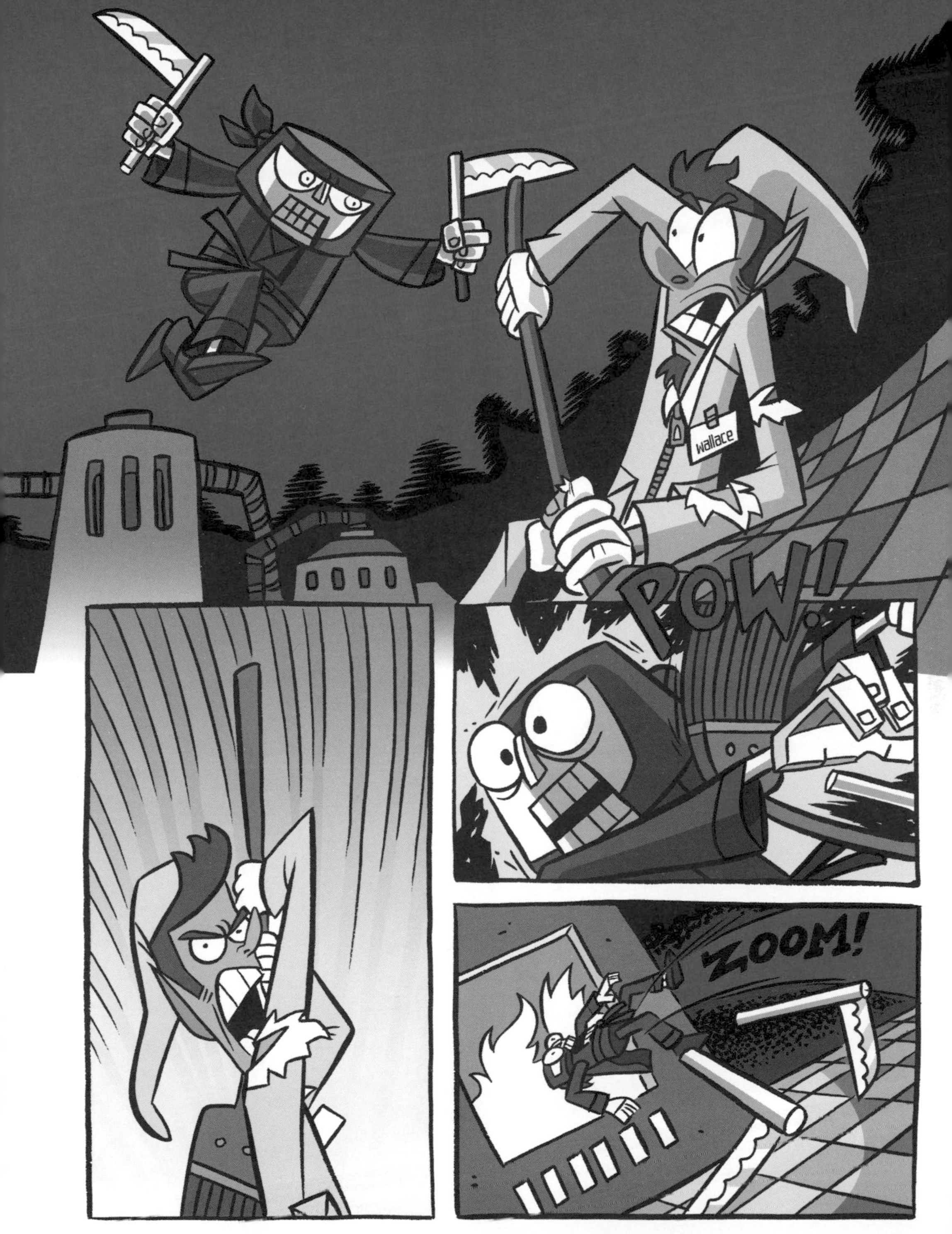

Wallace
POW!
ZOOM!

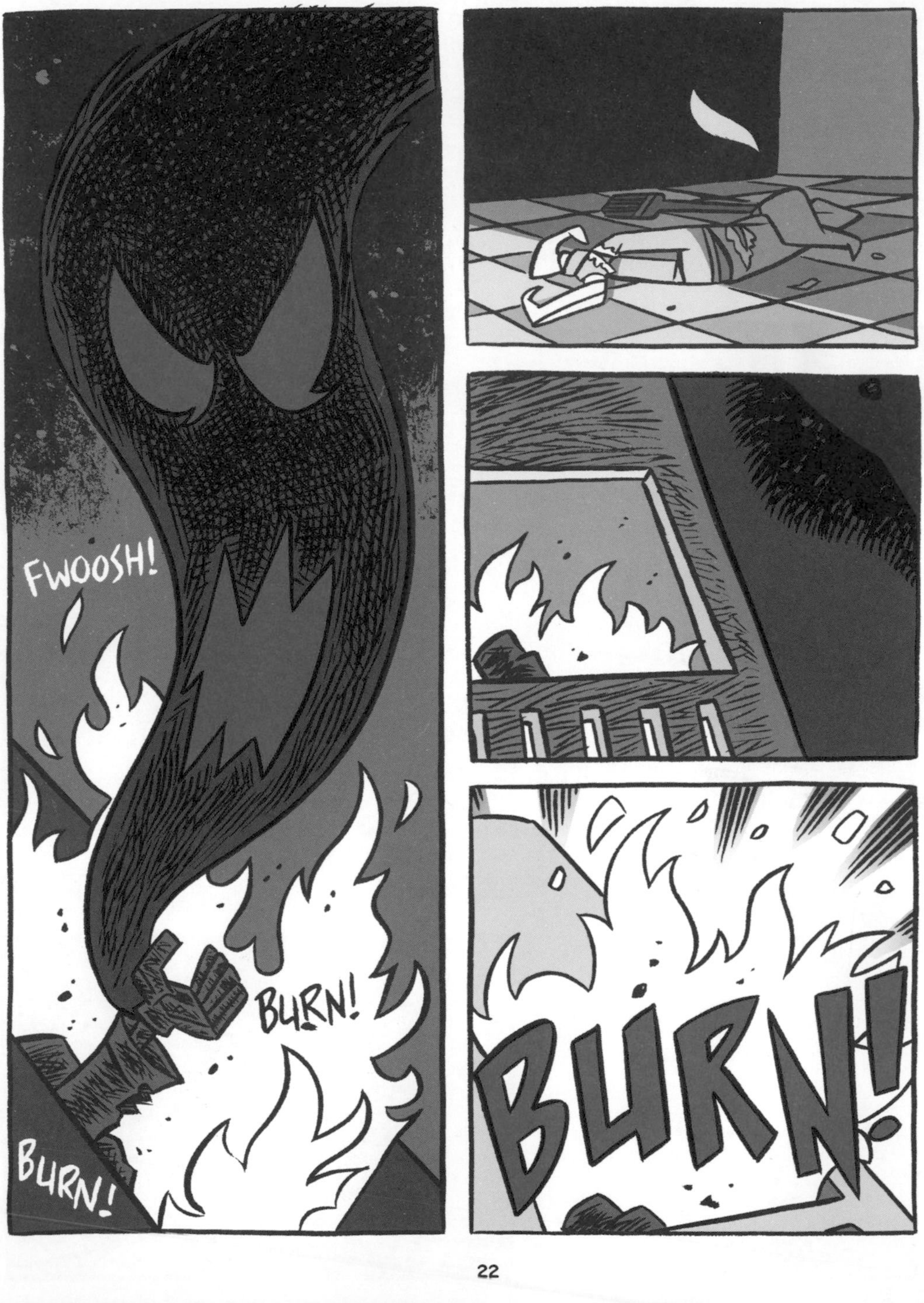
FWOOSH!
BURN!
BURN!
BURN!

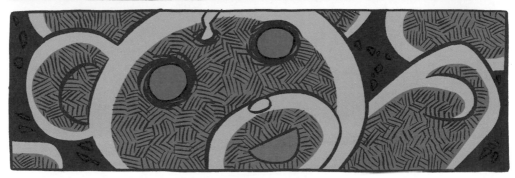

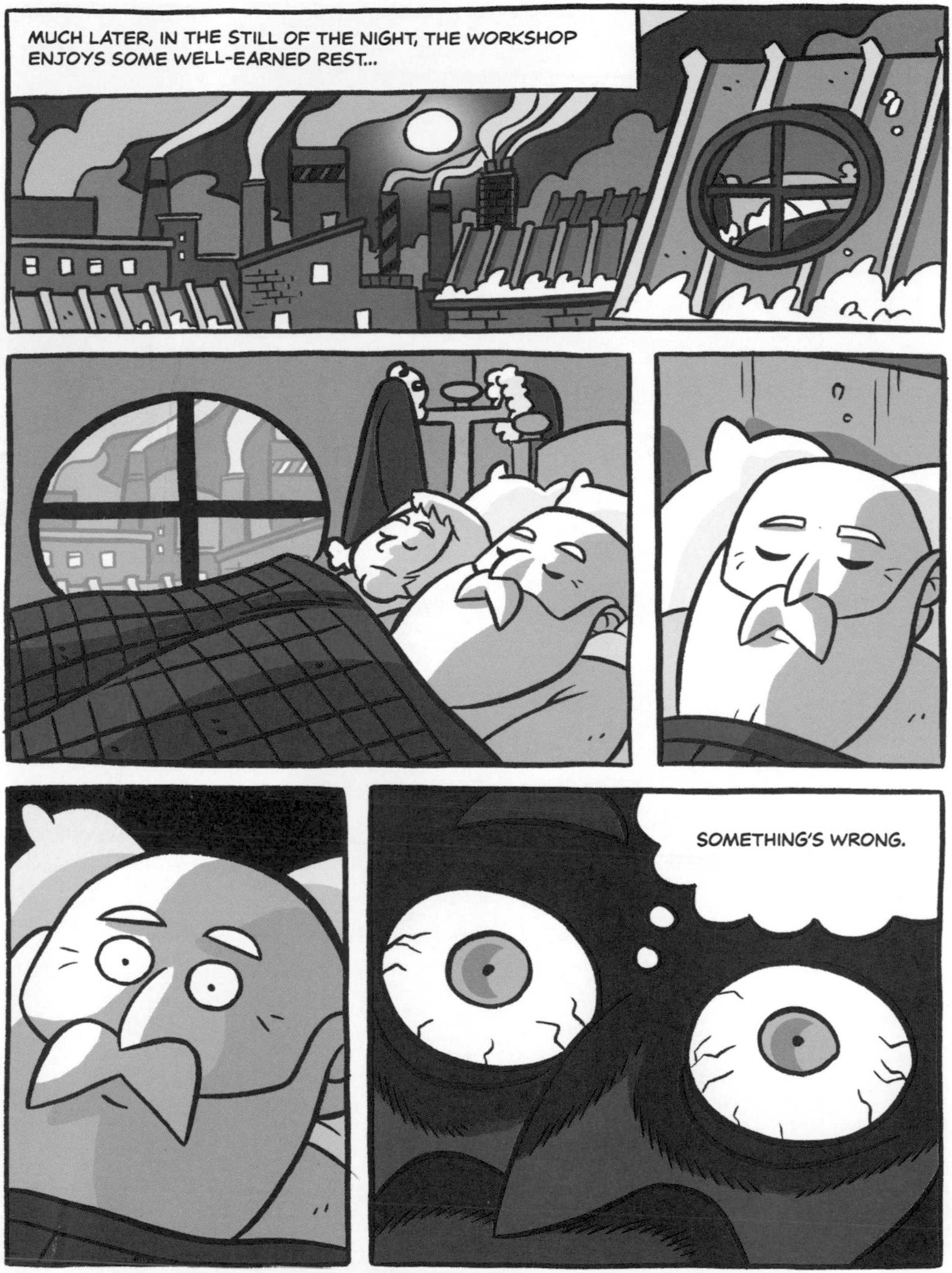
MUCH LATER, IN THE STILL OF THE NIGHT, THE WORKSHOP ENJOYS SOME WELL-EARNED REST...
SOMETHING'S WRONG.

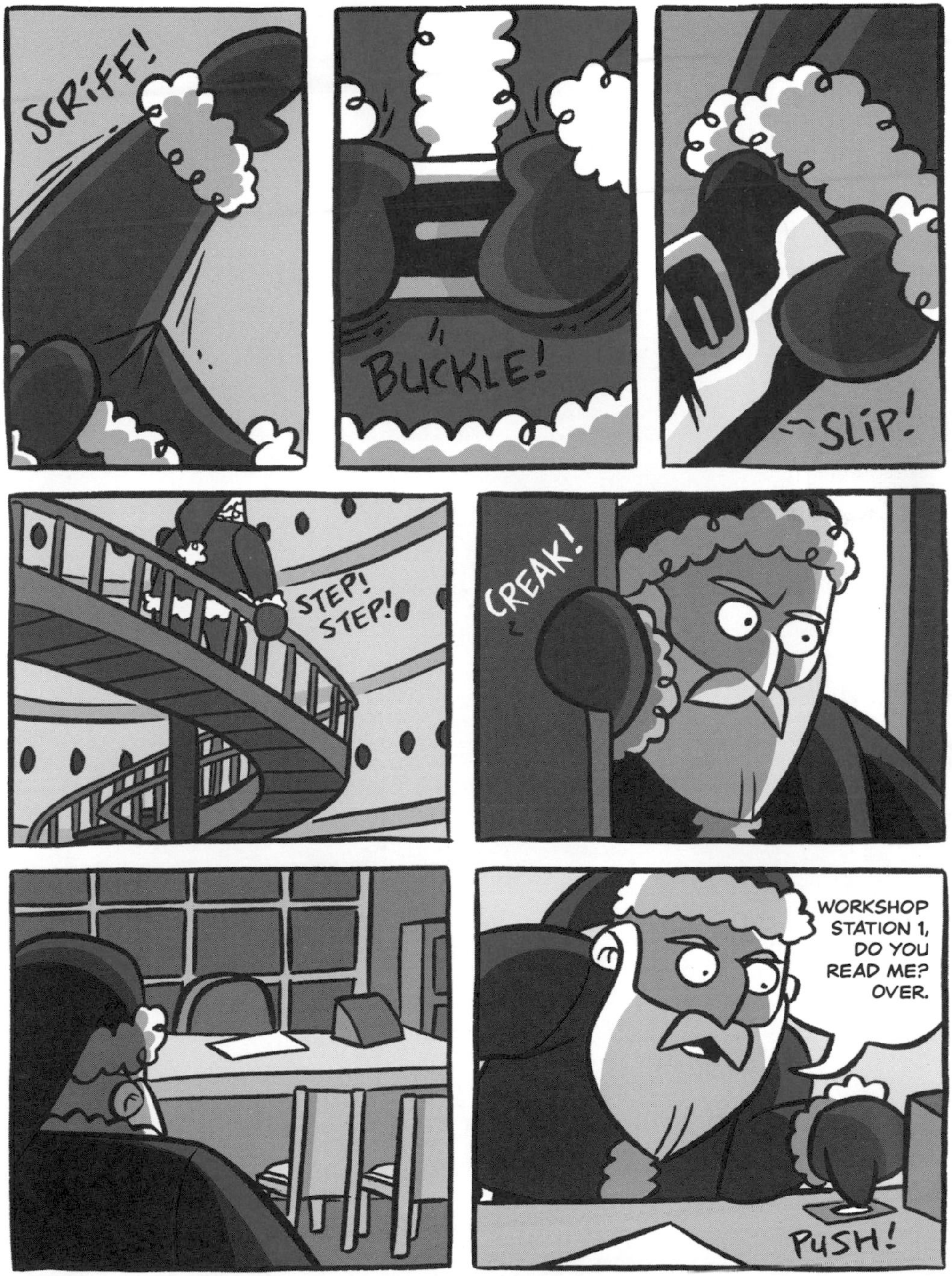
SCRIFF!
BUCKLE!
SLIP!
STEP! STEP!
CREAK!
WORKSHOP STATION 1, DO YOU READ ME? OVER.
PUSH!

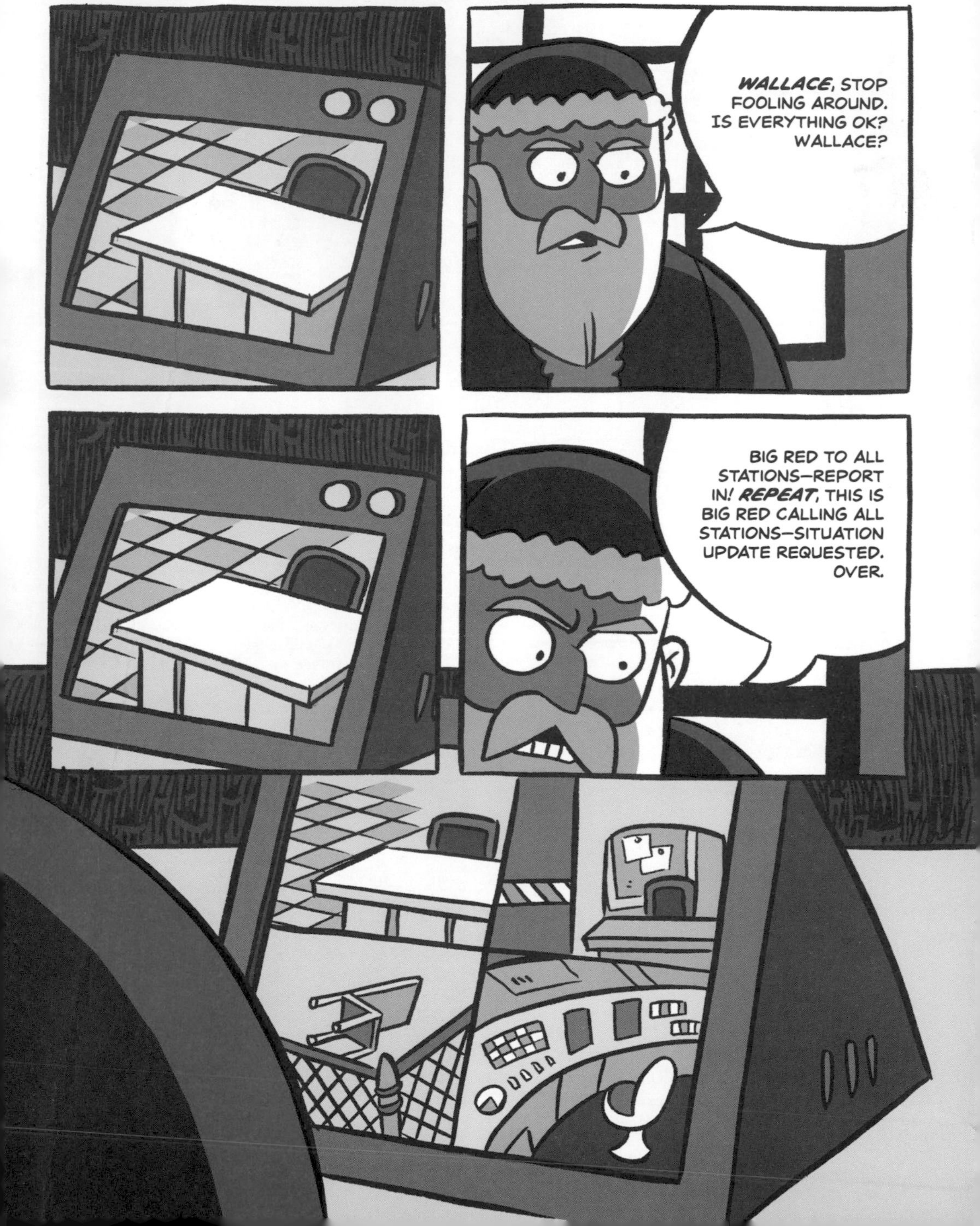
WALLACE, STOP FOOLING AROUND. IS EVERYTHING OK? WALLACE?
BIG RED TO ALL STATIONS—REPORT IN! *REPEAT*, THIS IS BIG RED CALLING ALL STATIONS—SITUATION UPDATE REQUESTED. OVER.

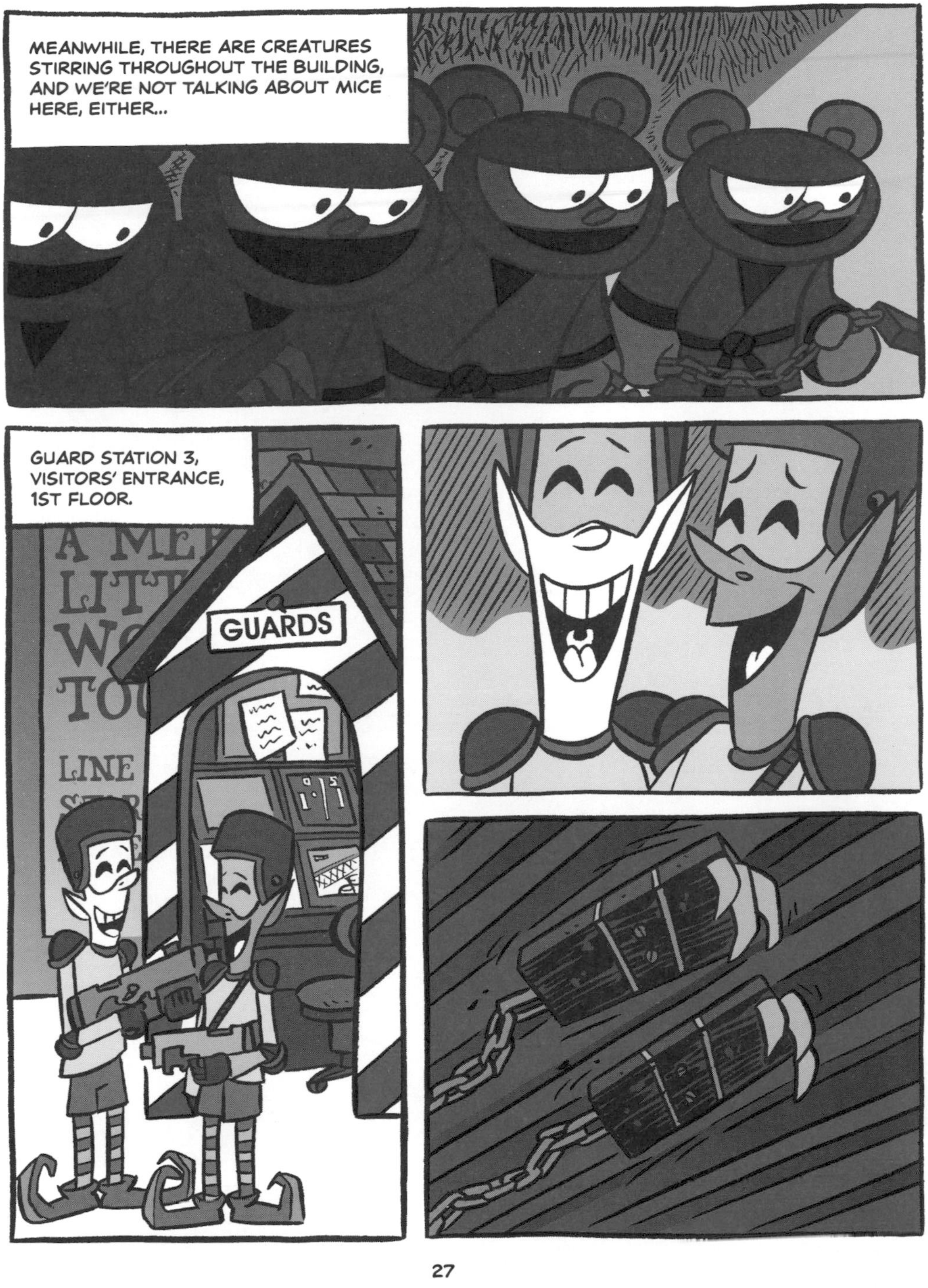
MEANWHILE, THERE ARE CREATURES STIRRING THROUGHOUT THE BUILDING, AND WE'RE NOT TALKING ABOUT MICE HERE, EITHER...
GUARD STATION 3, VISITORS' ENTRANCE, 1ST FLOOR.
GUARDS

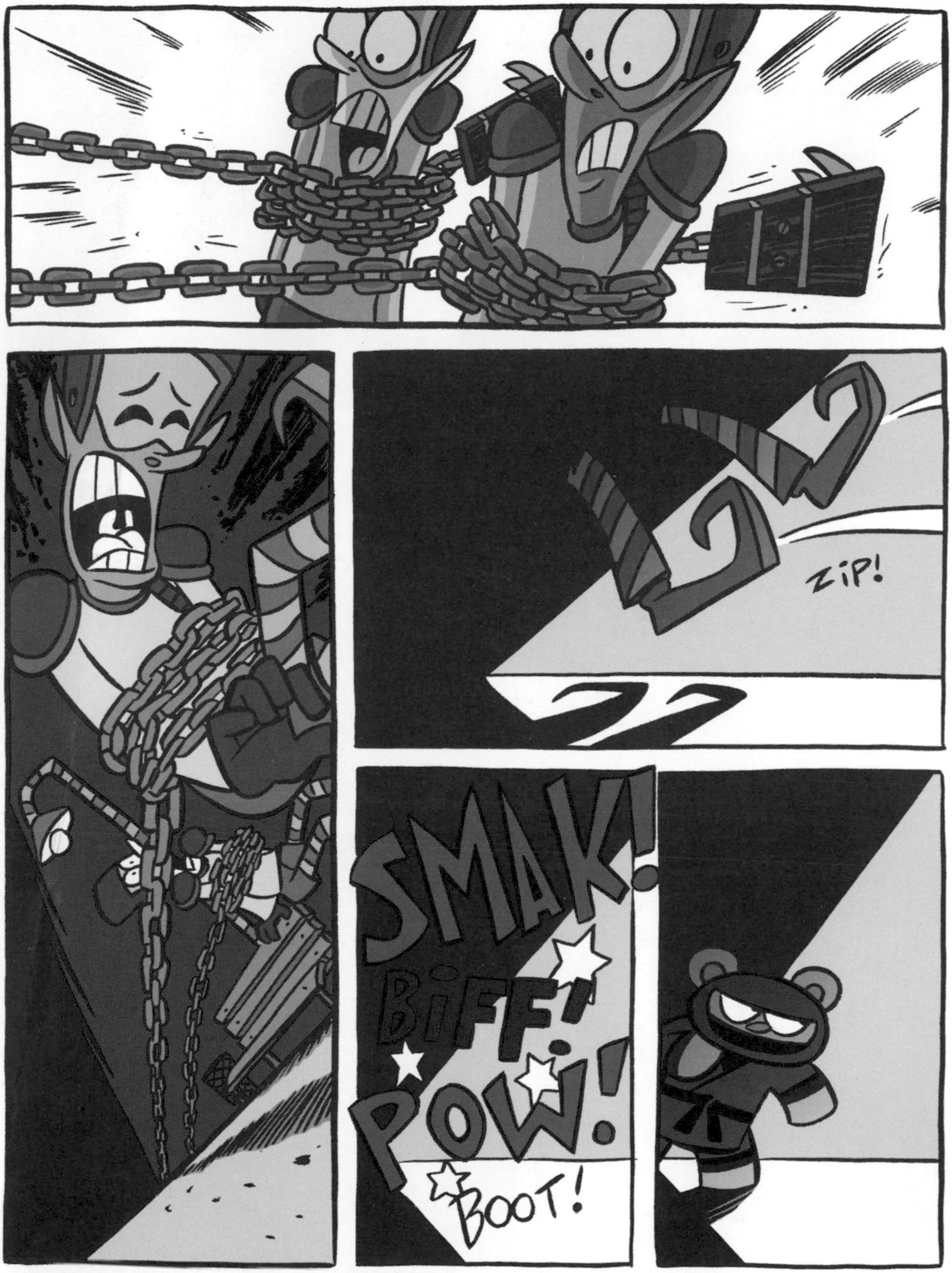
ZIP!
SMAK!
BIFF!
POW!
BOOT!

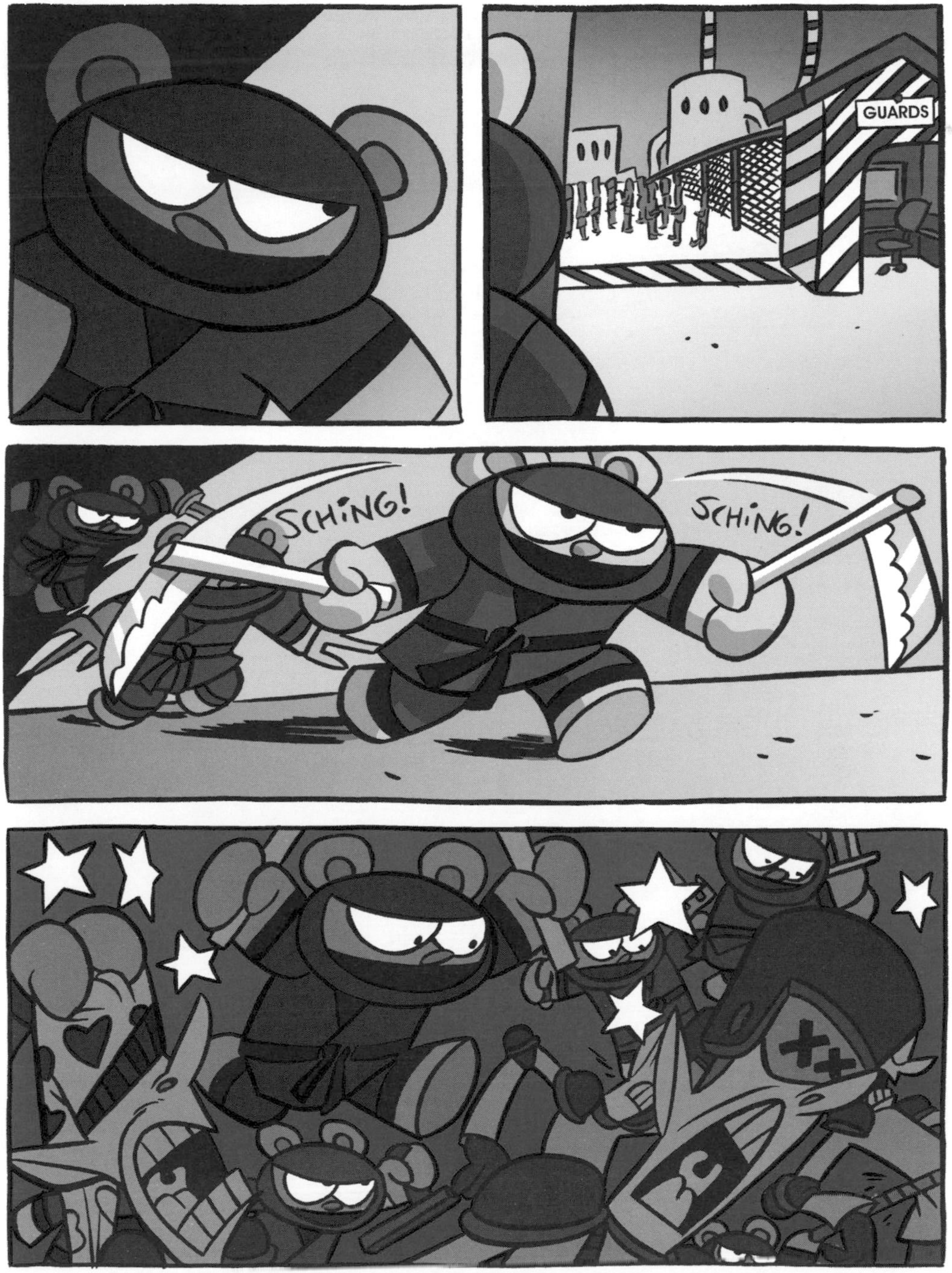
GUARDS
SCHING!
SCHING!

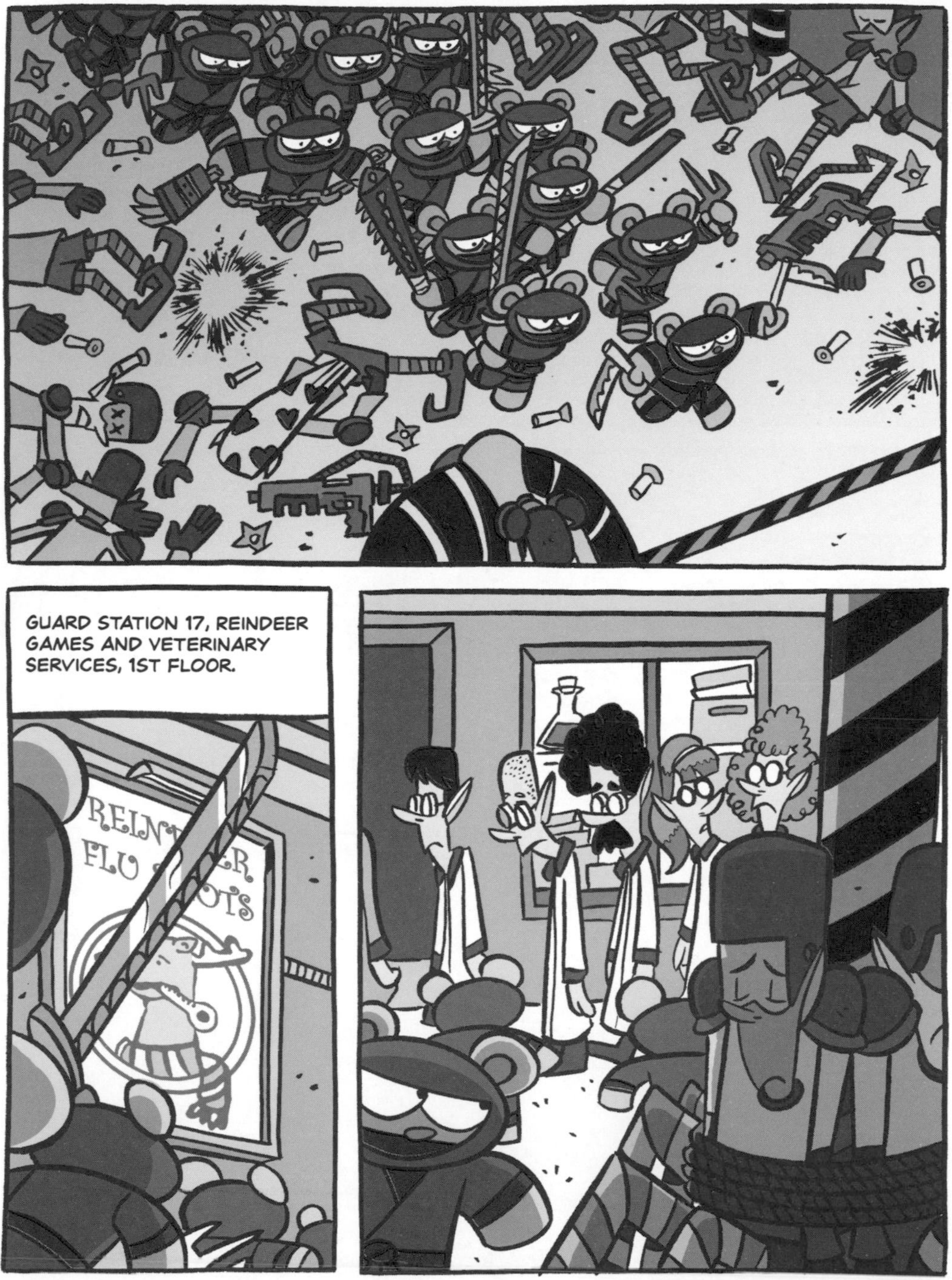
GUARD STATION 17, REINDEER GAMES AND VETERINARY SERVICES, 1ST FLOOR.

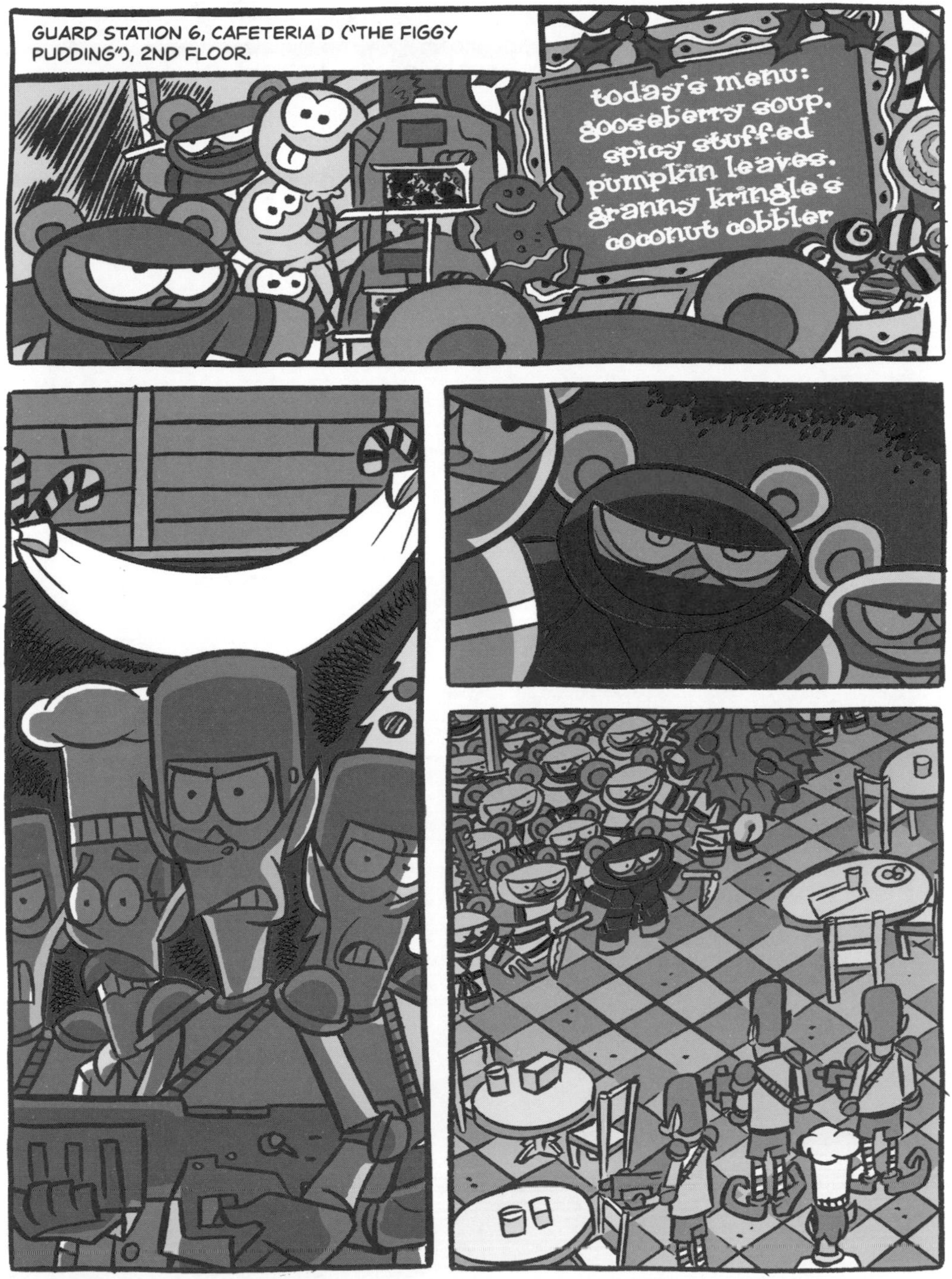
GUARD STATION 6, CAFETERIA D ("THE FIGGY PUDDING"), 2ND FLOOR.
today's menu: gooseberry soup. spicy stuffed pumpkin leaves. pumpkin kringle's granny kringle's coconut cobbler

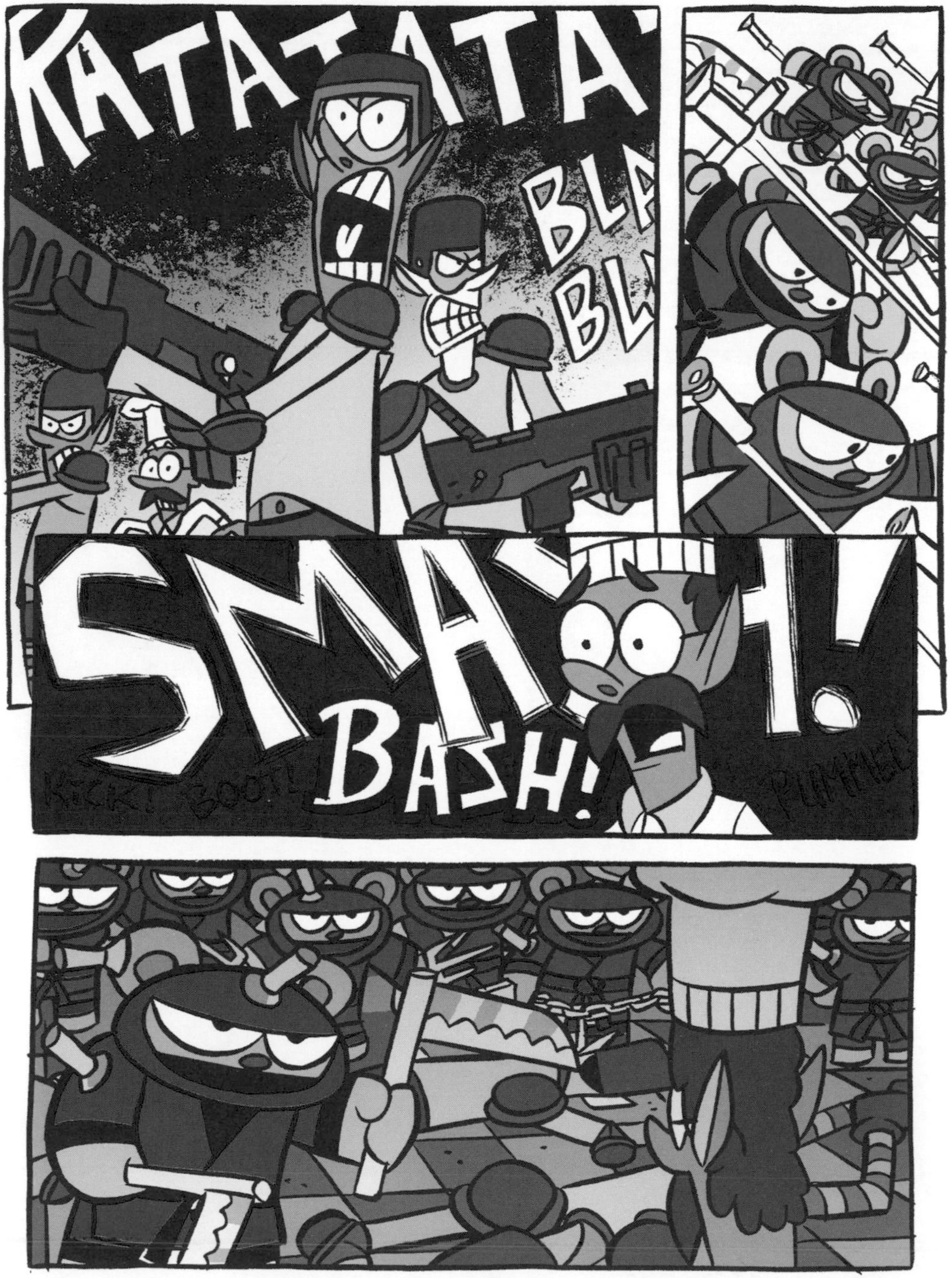
KATATATA
BLA
BL
SMASH!
BASH!
KICK!
BOOT!
PUMMEL!

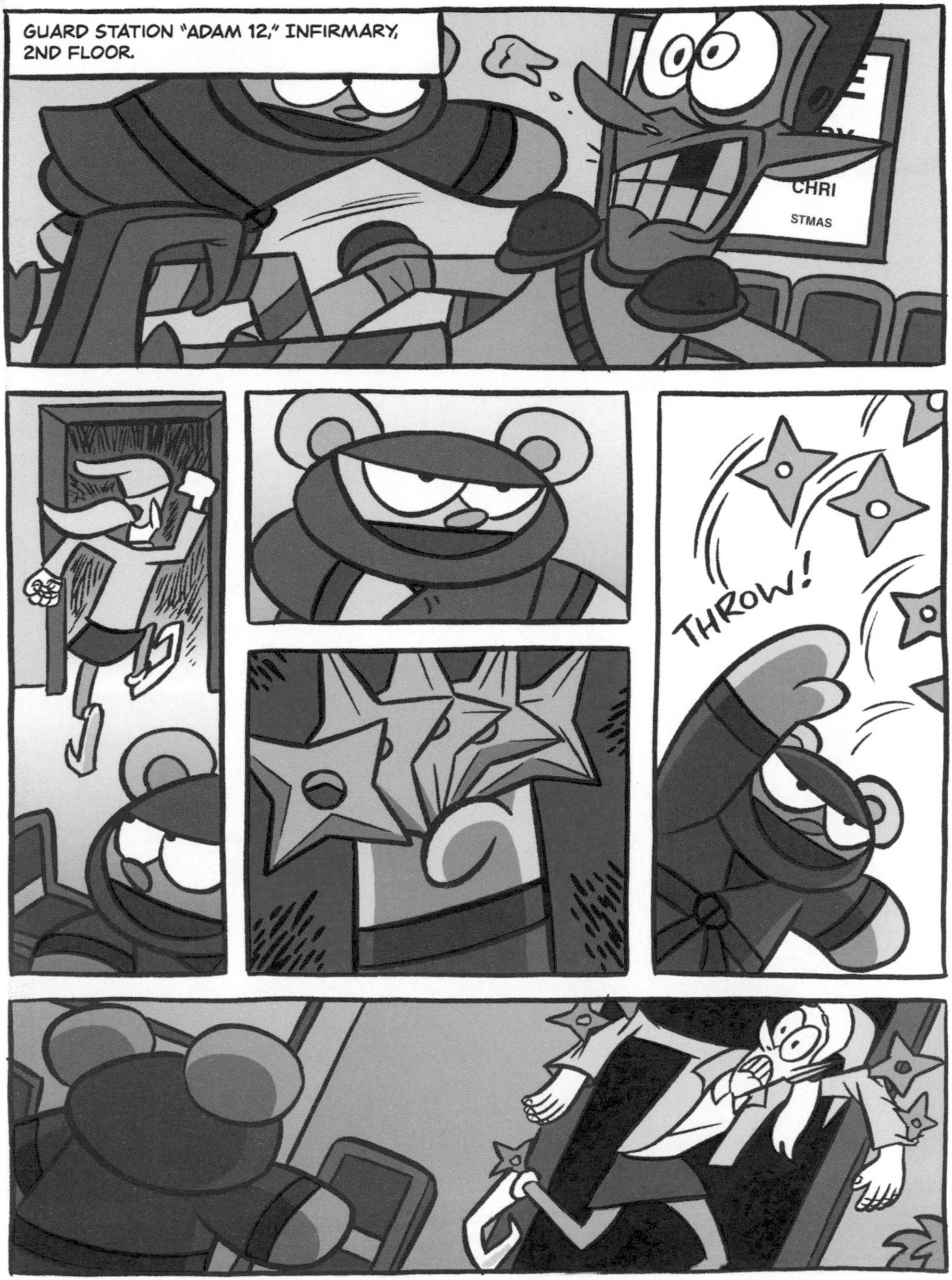
GUARD STATION "ADAM 12," INFIRMARY, 2ND FLOOR.
CHRI
STMAS
THROW!

ELF DORMITORY A6 ("THE MISTLETOE MANIACS"), RESIDENTIAL WING, 3RD FLOOR.

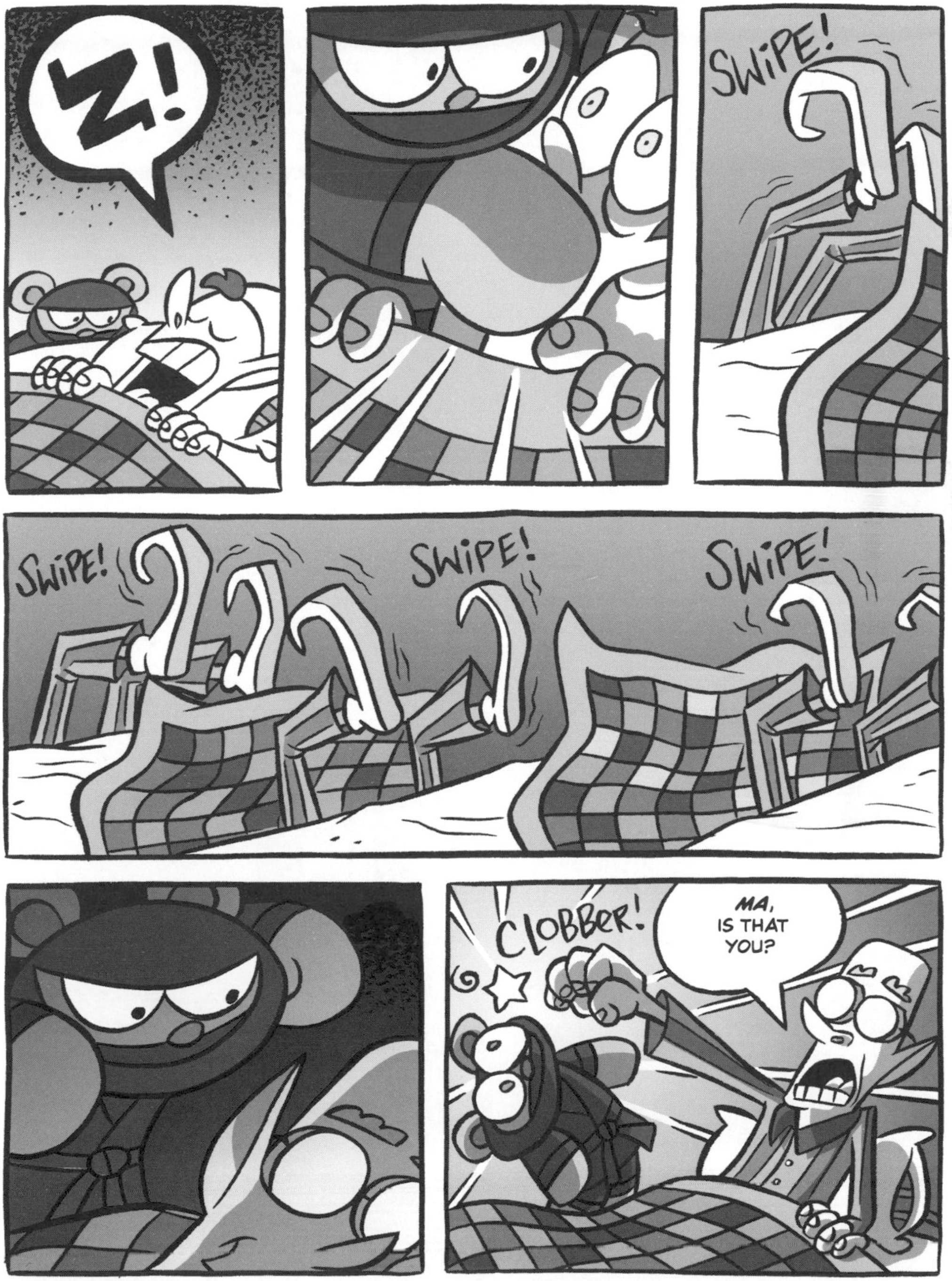
Z!
SWIPE!
SWIPE!
SWIPE!
SWIPE!
CLOBBER!
MA, IS THAT YOU?

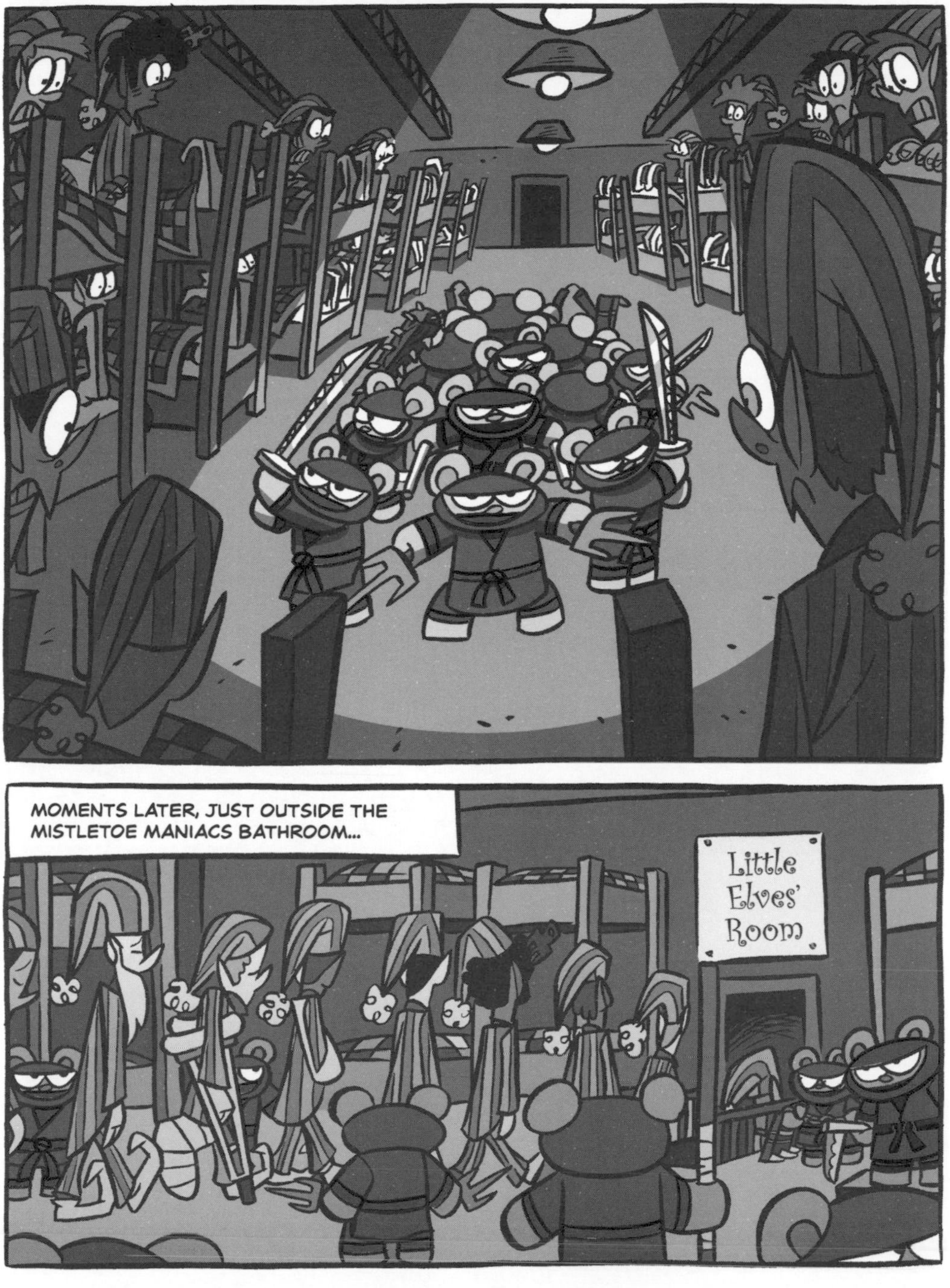
MOMENTS LATER, JUST OUTSIDE THE MISTLETOE MANIACS BATHROOM...
Little Elves' Room

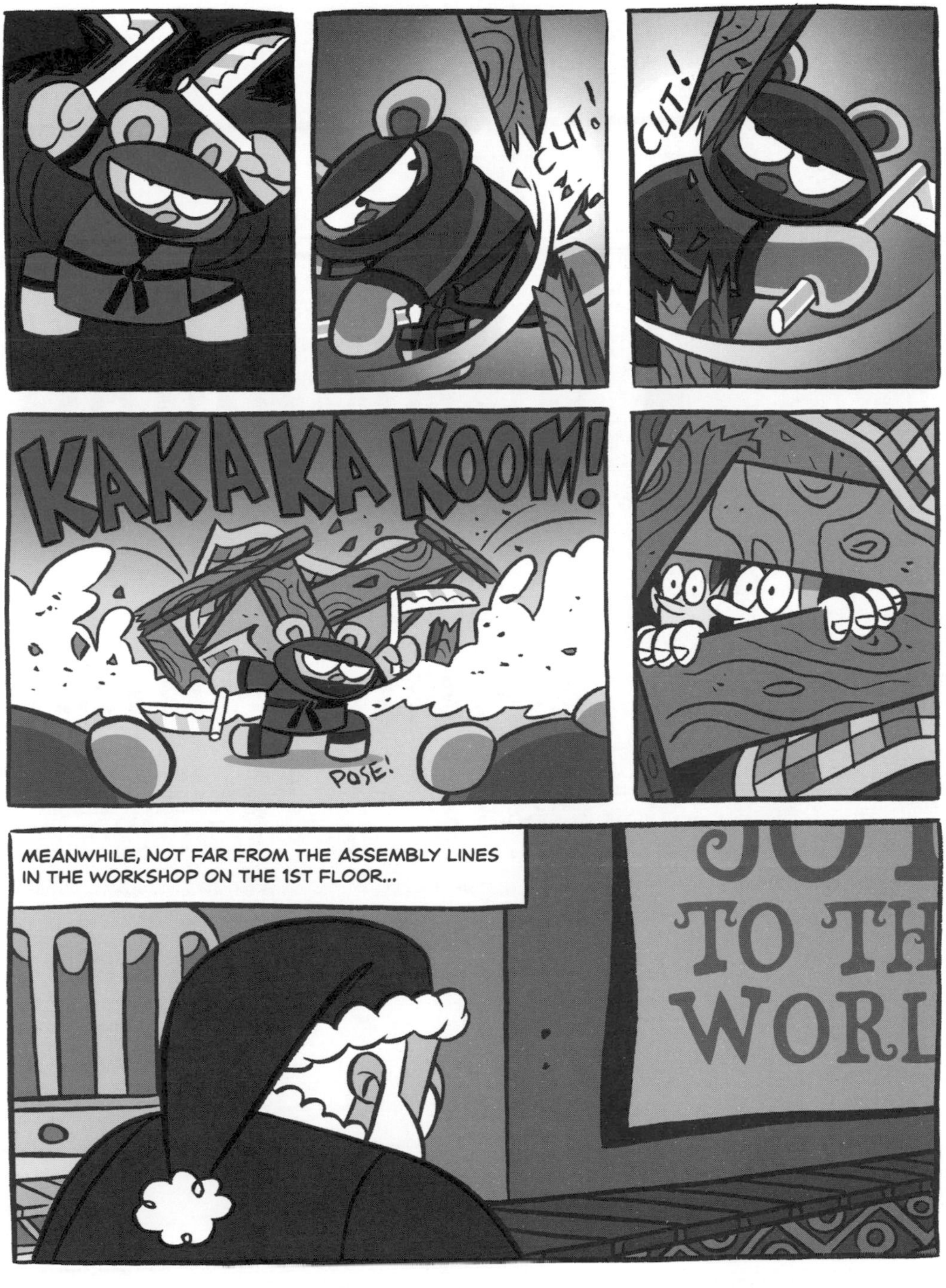
CUT!
CUT!
KAKAKAKOOM!
POSE!
MEANWHILE, NOT FAR FROM THE ASSEMBLY LINES IN THE WORKSHOP ON THE 1ST FLOOR...
TO TH
WORL

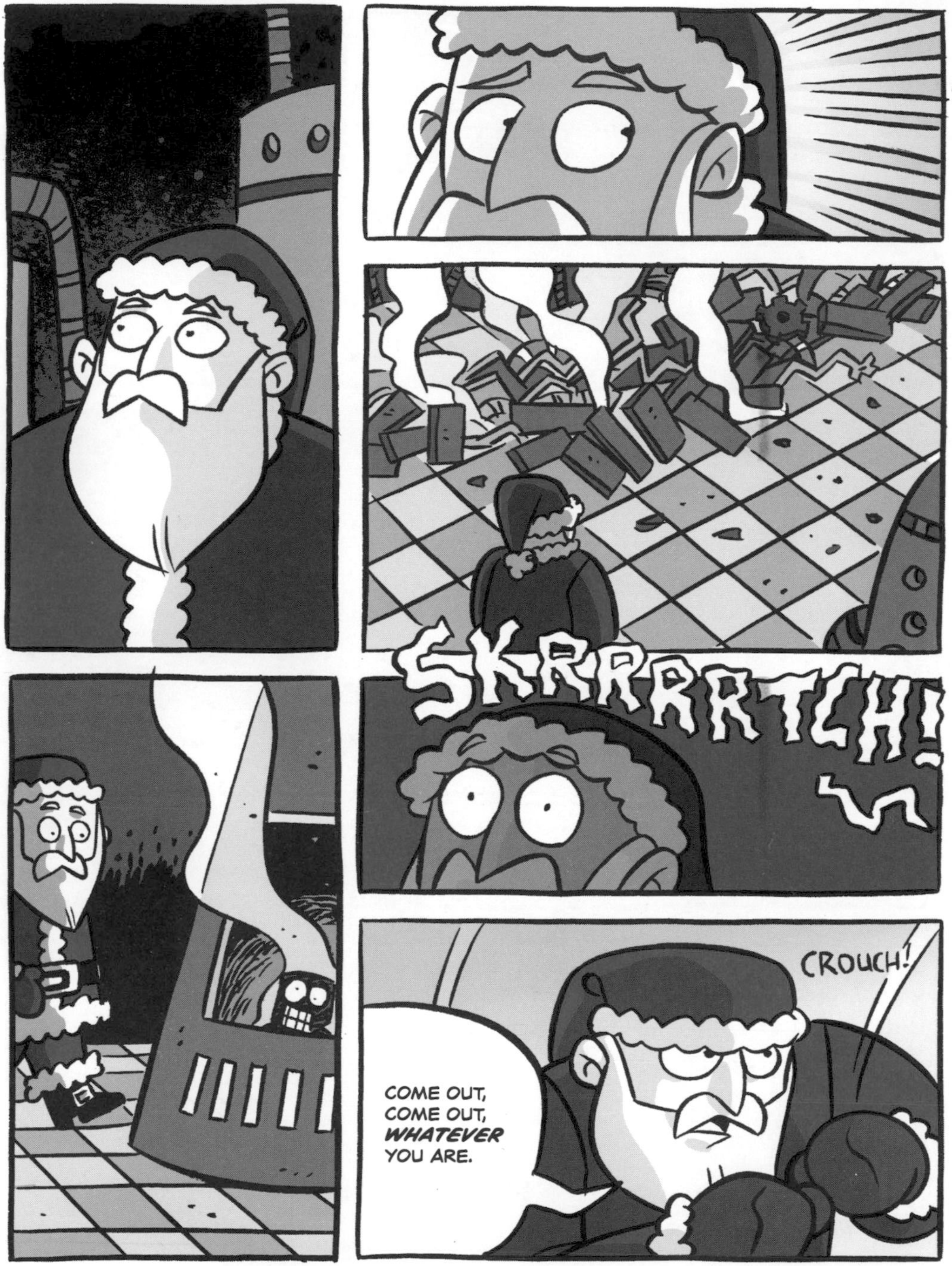
SKRRRRTCH!
CROUCH!
COME OUT,
COME OUT,
WHATEVER
YOU ARE.

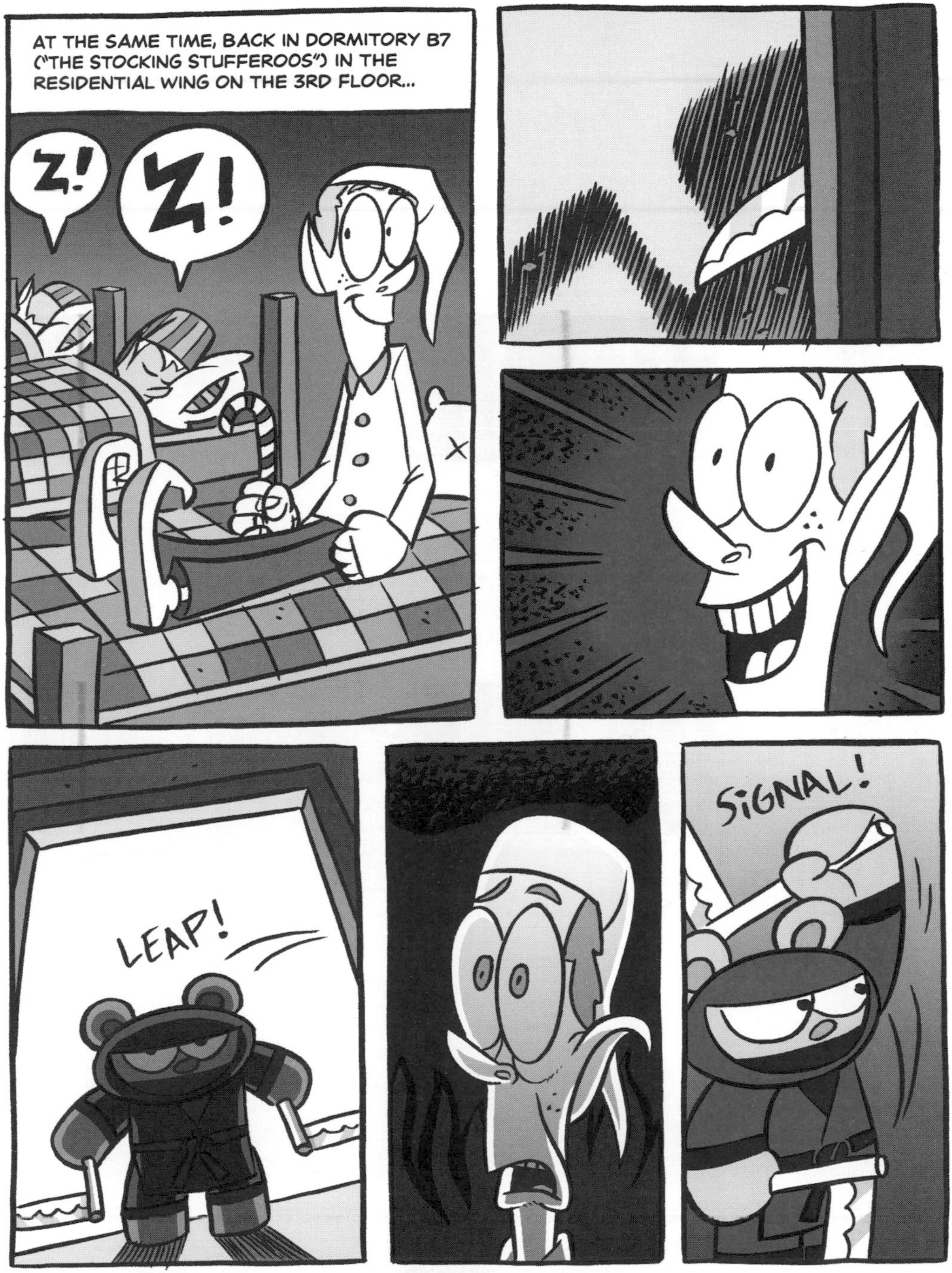
AT THE SAME TIME, BACK IN DORMITORY B7 ("THE STOCKING STUFFEROOS") IN THE RESIDENTIAL WING ON THE 3RD FLOOR...
Z!
Z!
LEAP!
SIGNAL!

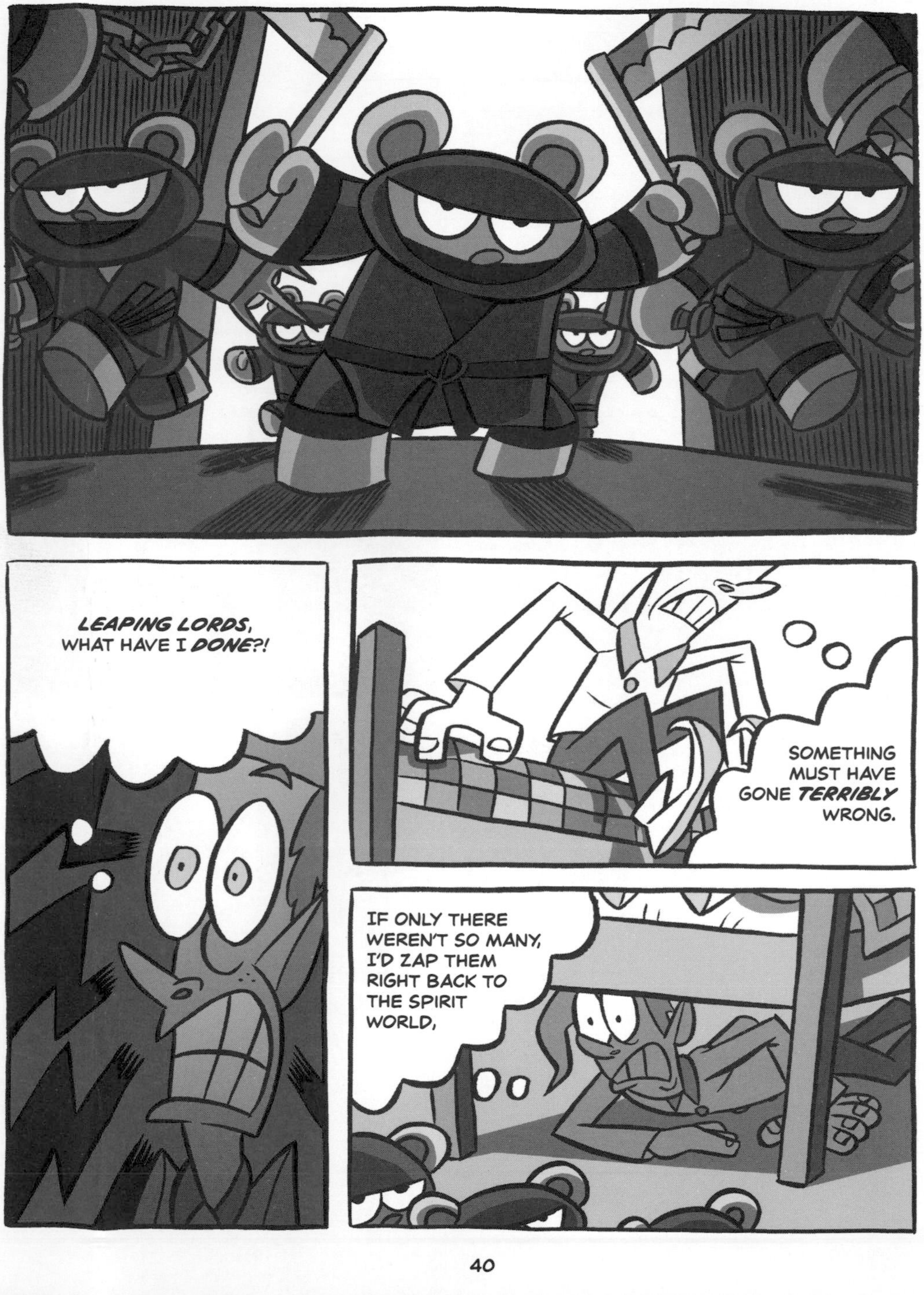
LEAPING LORDS, WHAT HAVE I *DONE*?!
SOMETHING MUST HAVE GONE *TERRIBLY* WRONG.
IF ONLY THERE WEREN'T SO MANY, I'D ZAP THEM RIGHT BACK TO THE SPIRIT WORLD,

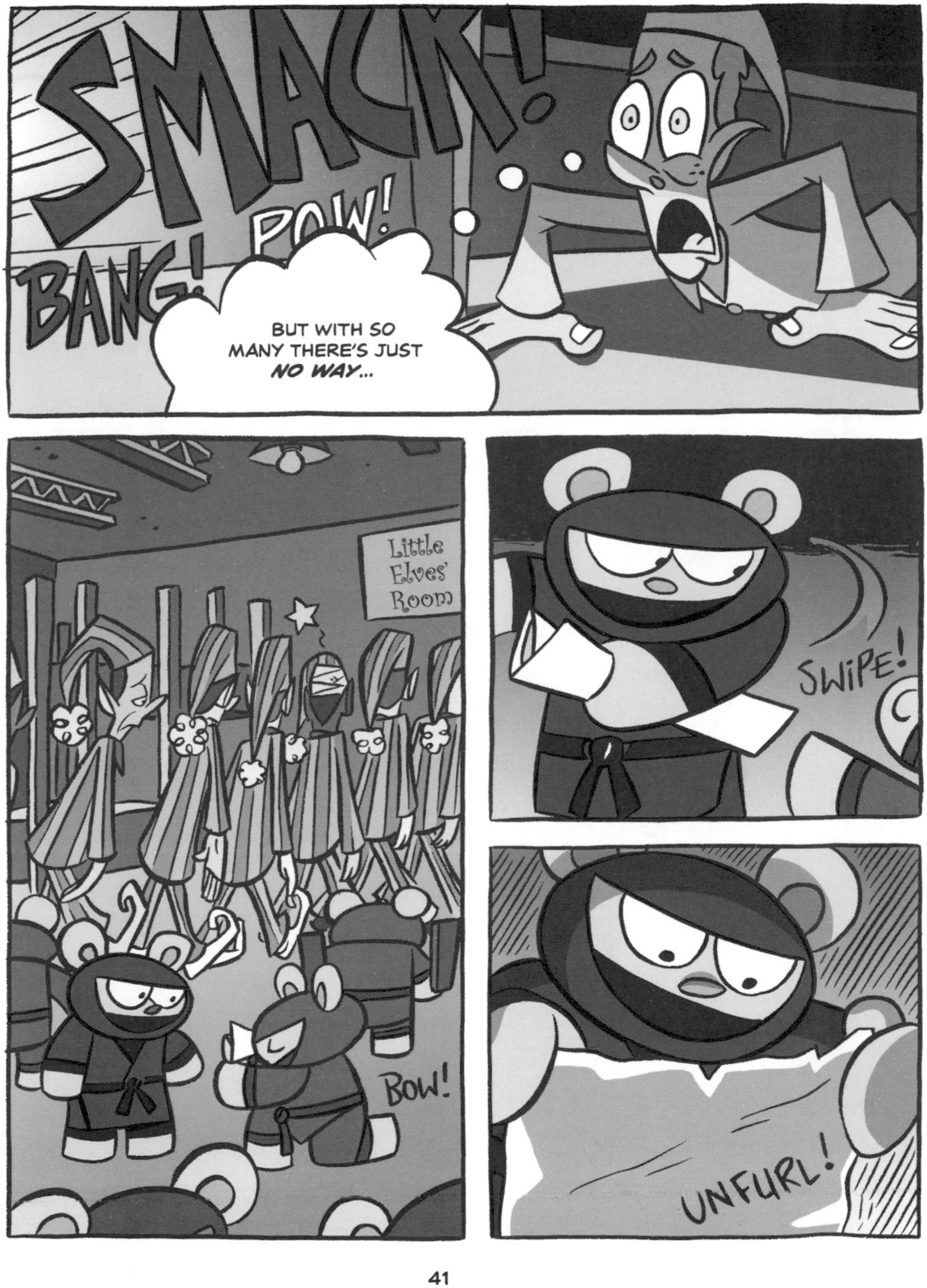
SMACK!
BANG!
POW!
BUT WITH SO MANY THERE'S JUST *NO WAY*...
Little Elves' Room
BOW!
SWIPE!
UNFURL!

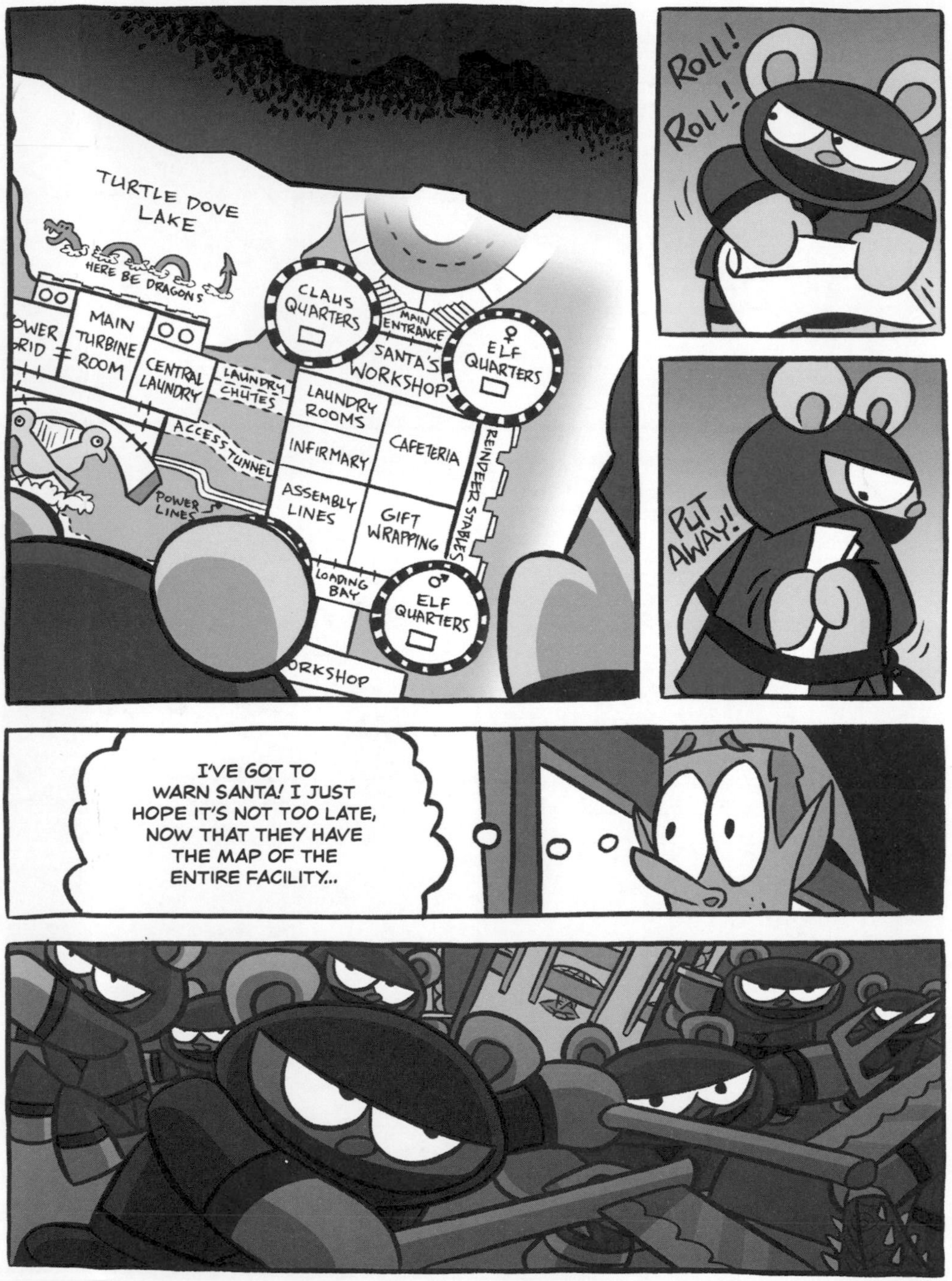
TURTLE DOVE LAKE
HERE BE DRAGONS
CLAUS QUARTERS
MAIN ENTRANCE
ELF QUARTERS
MAIN TURBINE ROOM
CENTRAL LAUNDRY
LAUNDRY CHUTES
SANTA'S WORKSHOP
LAUNDRY ROOMS
INFIRMARY
CAFETERIA
ACCESS TUNNEL
ASSEMBLY LINES
GIFT WRAPPING
REINDEER STABLES
POWER LINES
LOADING BAY
ELF QUARTERS
ORKSHOP
ROLL! ROLL!
PUT AWAY!
I'VE GOT TO WARN SANTA! I JUST HOPE IT'S NOT TOO LATE, NOW THAT THEY HAVE THE MAP OF THE ENTIRE FACILITY...

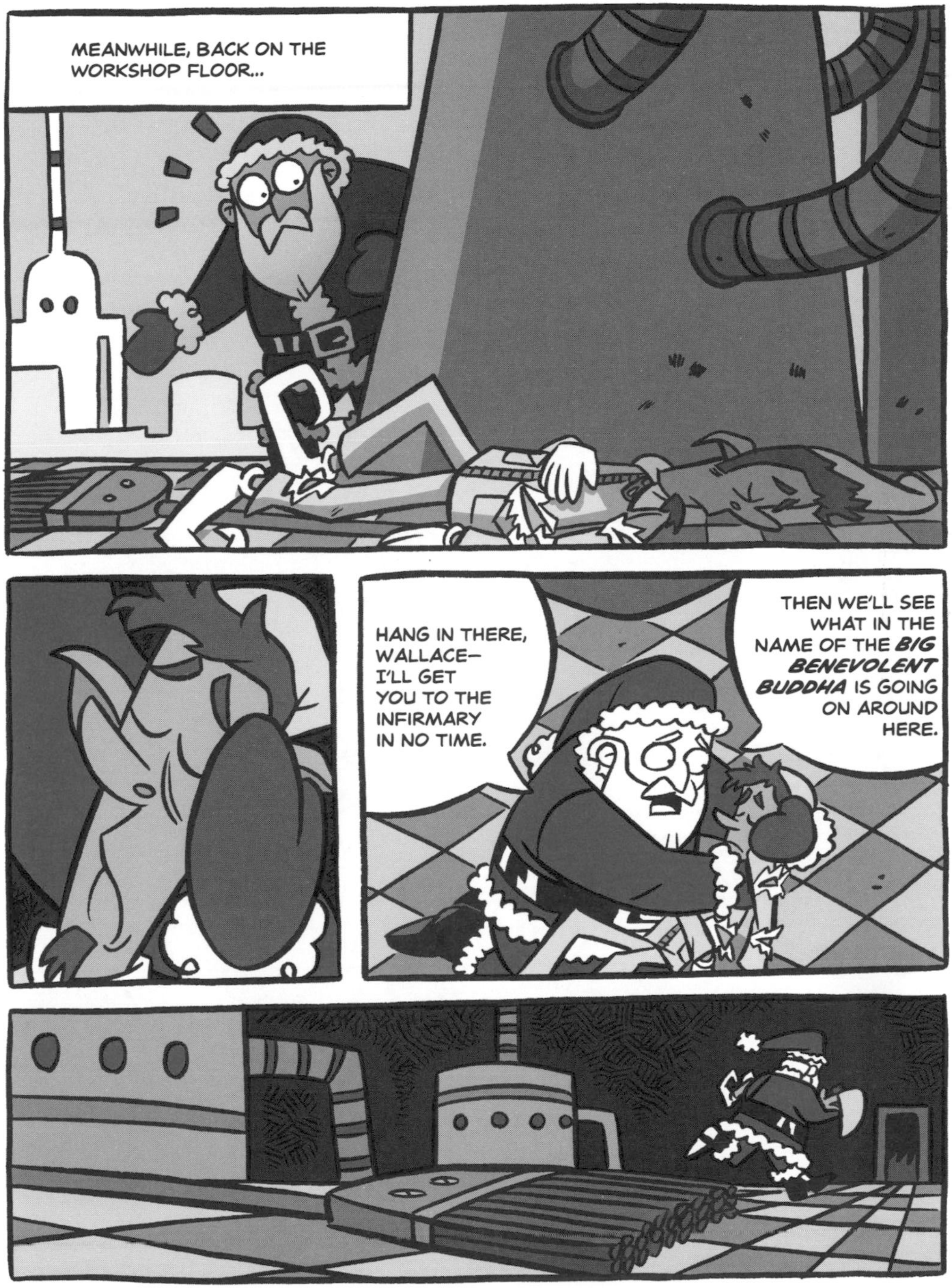
MEANWHILE, BACK ON THE WORKSHOP FLOOR...
HANG IN THERE, WALLACE— I'LL GET YOU TO THE INFIRMARY IN NO TIME.
THEN WE'LL SEE WHAT IN THE NAME OF THE *BIG BENEVOLENT BUDDHA* IS GOING ON AROUND HERE.

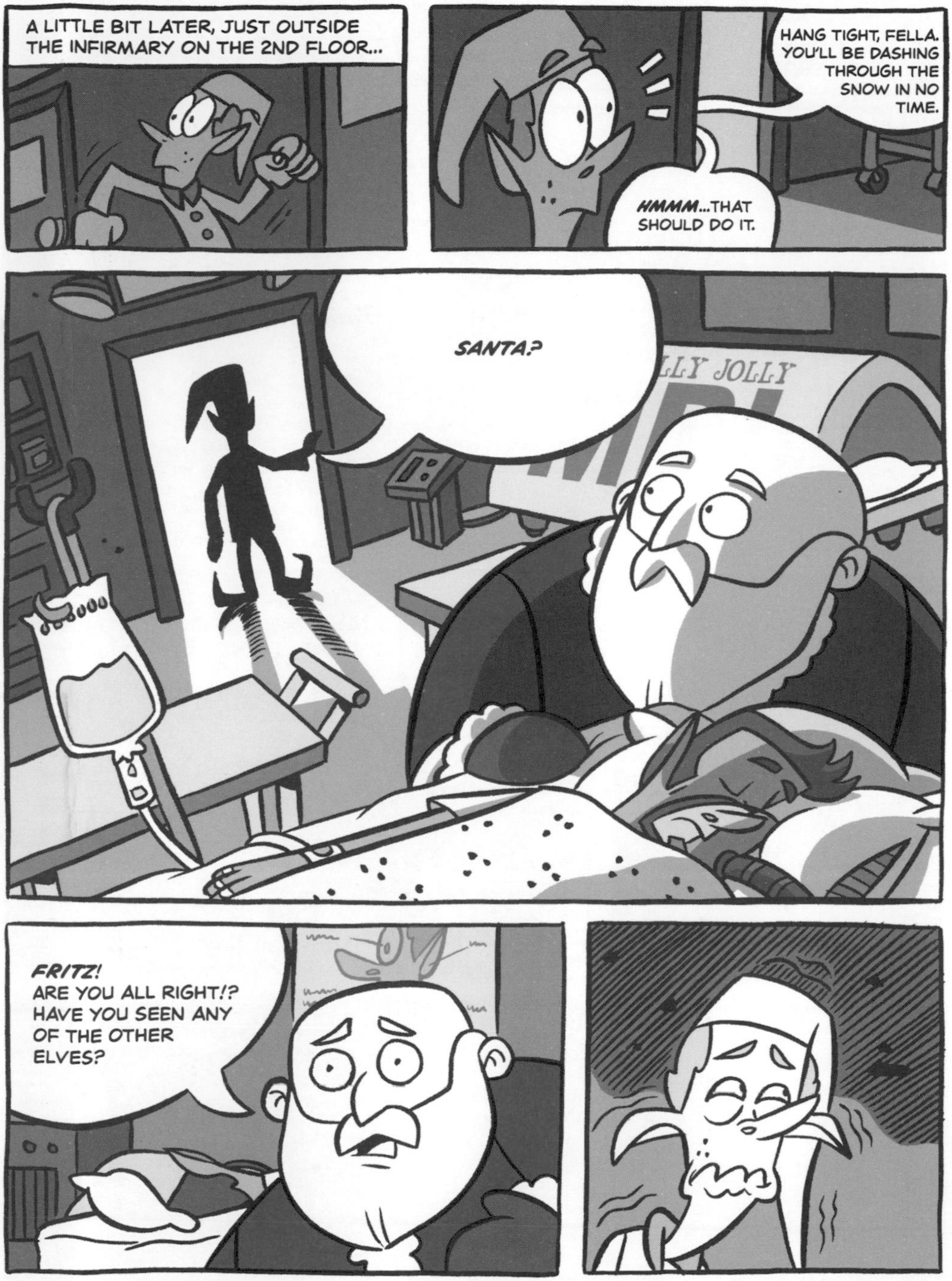
A LITTLE BIT LATER, JUST OUTSIDE THE INFIRMARY ON THE 2ND FLOOR...
HANG TIGHT, FELLA. YOU'LL BE DASHING THROUGH THE SNOW IN NO TIME.
HMMM...THAT SHOULD DO IT.
SANTA?
FRITZ! ARE YOU ALL RIGHT!? HAVE YOU SEEN ANY OF THE OTHER ELVES?

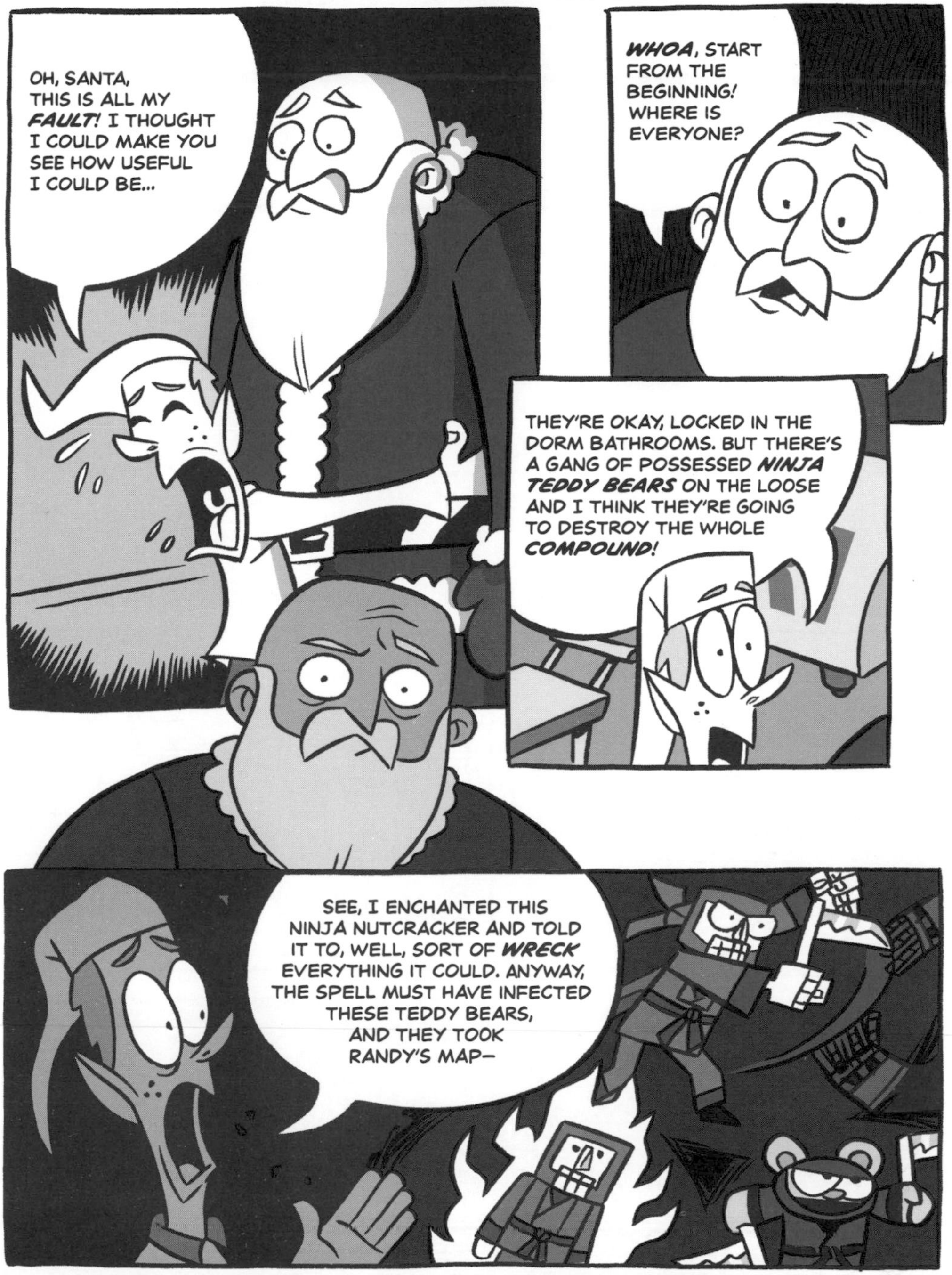

OH, SANTA, THIS IS ALL MY *FAULT!* I THOUGHT I COULD MAKE YOU SEE HOW USEFUL I COULD BE...
WHOA, START FROM THE BEGINNING! WHERE IS EVERYONE?
THEY'RE OKAY, LOCKED IN THE DORM BATHROOMS. BUT THERE'S A GANG OF POSSESSED *NINJA TEDDY BEARS* ON THE LOOSE AND I THINK THEY'RE GOING TO DESTROY THE WHOLE *COMPOUND!*
SEE, I ENCHANTED THIS NINJA NUTCRACKER AND TOLD IT TO, WELL, SORT OF *WRECK* EVERYTHING IT COULD. ANYWAY, THE SPELL MUST HAVE INFECTED THESE TEDDY BEARS, AND THEY TOOK RANDY'S MAP–

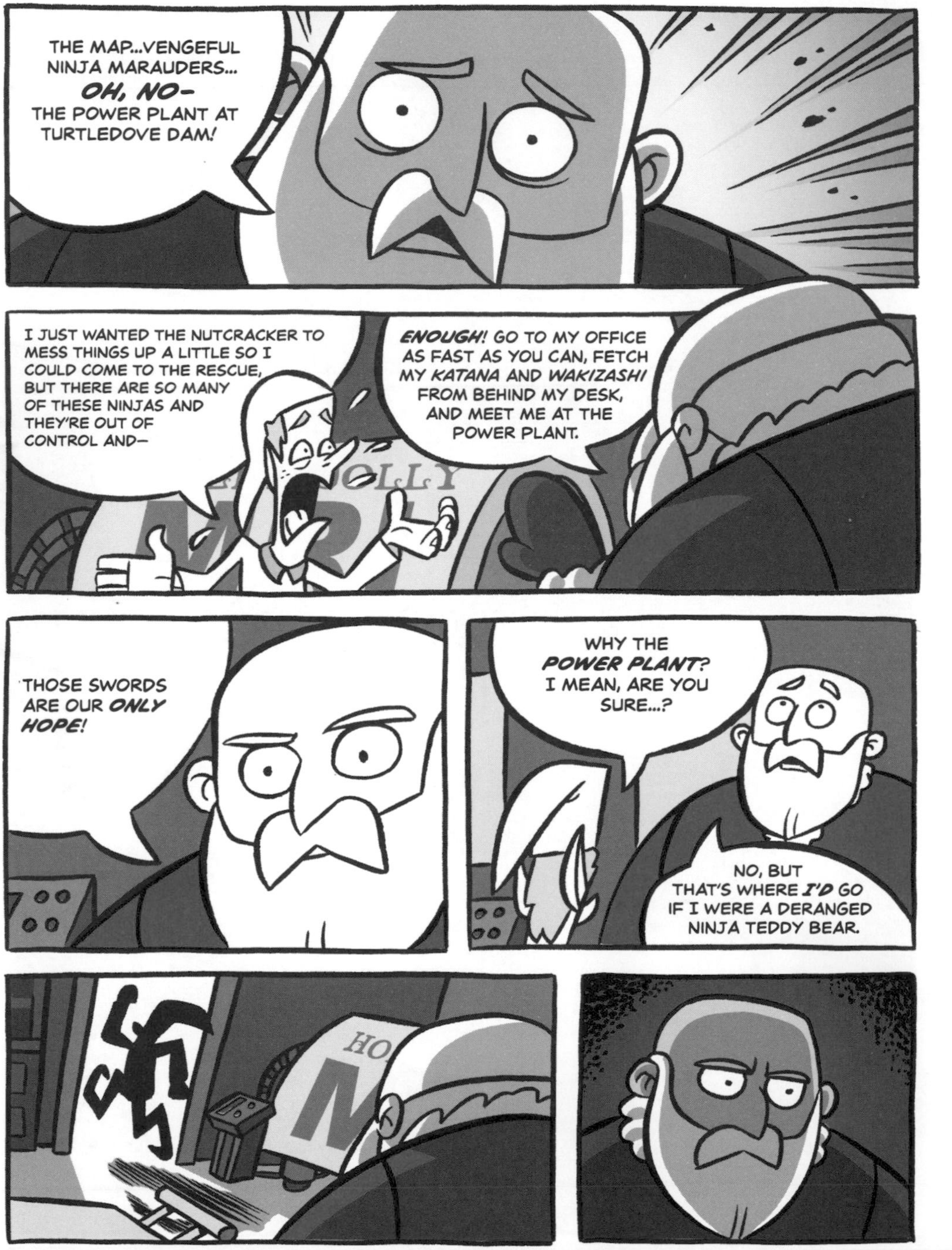
THE MAP...VENGEFUL NINJA MARAUDERS... OH, NO- THE POWER PLANT AT TURTLEDOVE DAM!
I JUST WANTED THE NUTCRACKER TO MESS THINGS UP A LITTLE SO I COULD COME TO THE RESCUE, BUT THERE ARE SO MANY OF THESE NINJAS AND THEY'RE OUT OF CONTROL AND—
ENOUGH! GO TO MY OFFICE AS FAST AS YOU CAN, FETCH MY KATANA AND WAKIZASHI FROM BEHIND MY DESK, AND MEET ME AT THE POWER PLANT.
THOSE SWORDS ARE OUR ONLY HOPE!
WHY THE POWER PLANT? I MEAN, ARE YOU SURE...?
NO, BUT THAT'S WHERE I'D GO IF I WERE A DERANGED NINJA TEDDY BEAR.

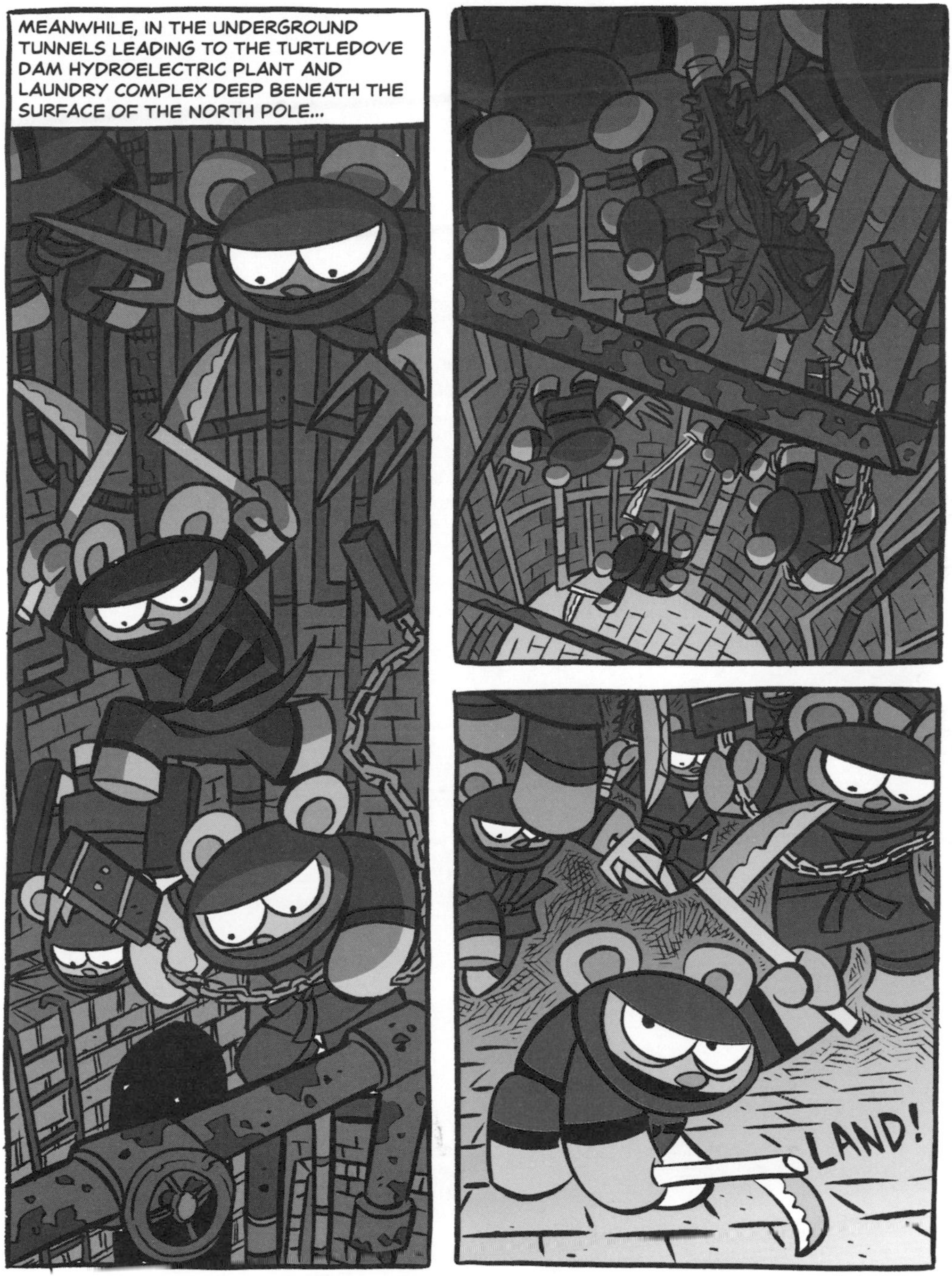
MEANWHILE, IN THE UNDERGROUND TUNNELS LEADING TO THE TURTLEDOVE DAM HYDROELECTRIC PLANT AND LAUNDRY COMPLEX DEEP BENEATH THE SURFACE OF THE NORTH POLE...
LAND!

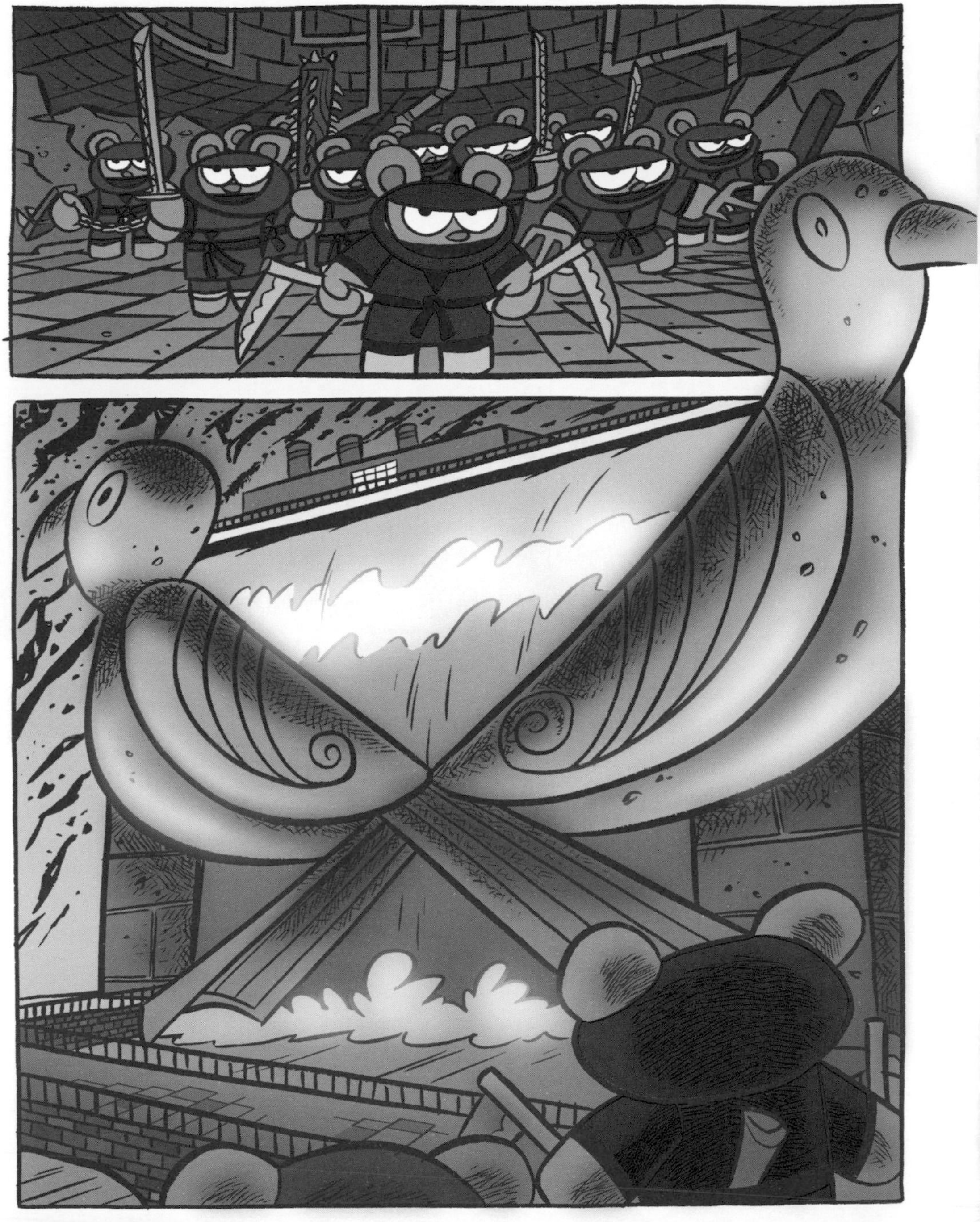

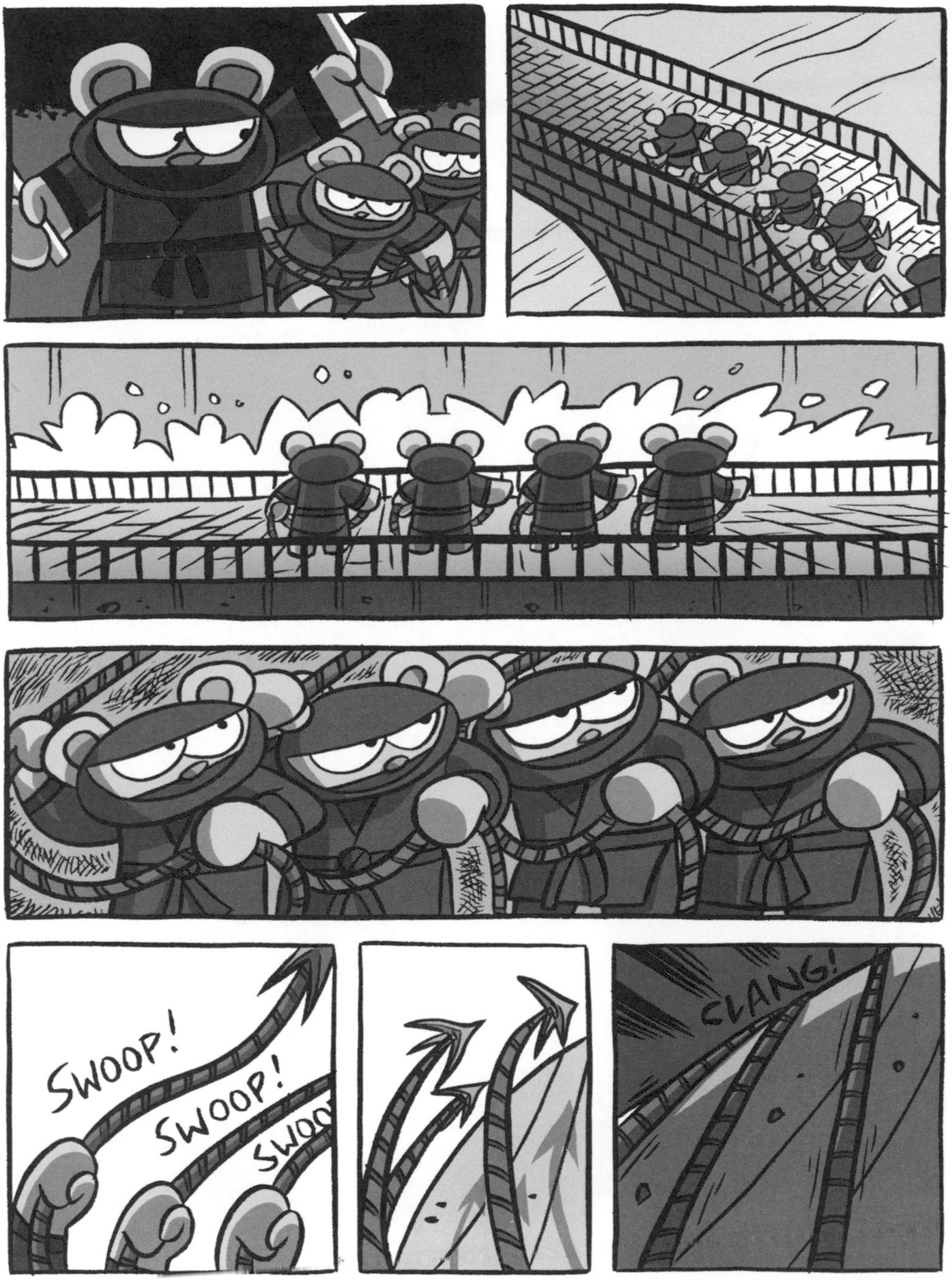
SWOOP!
SWOOP!
SWOO
CLANG!

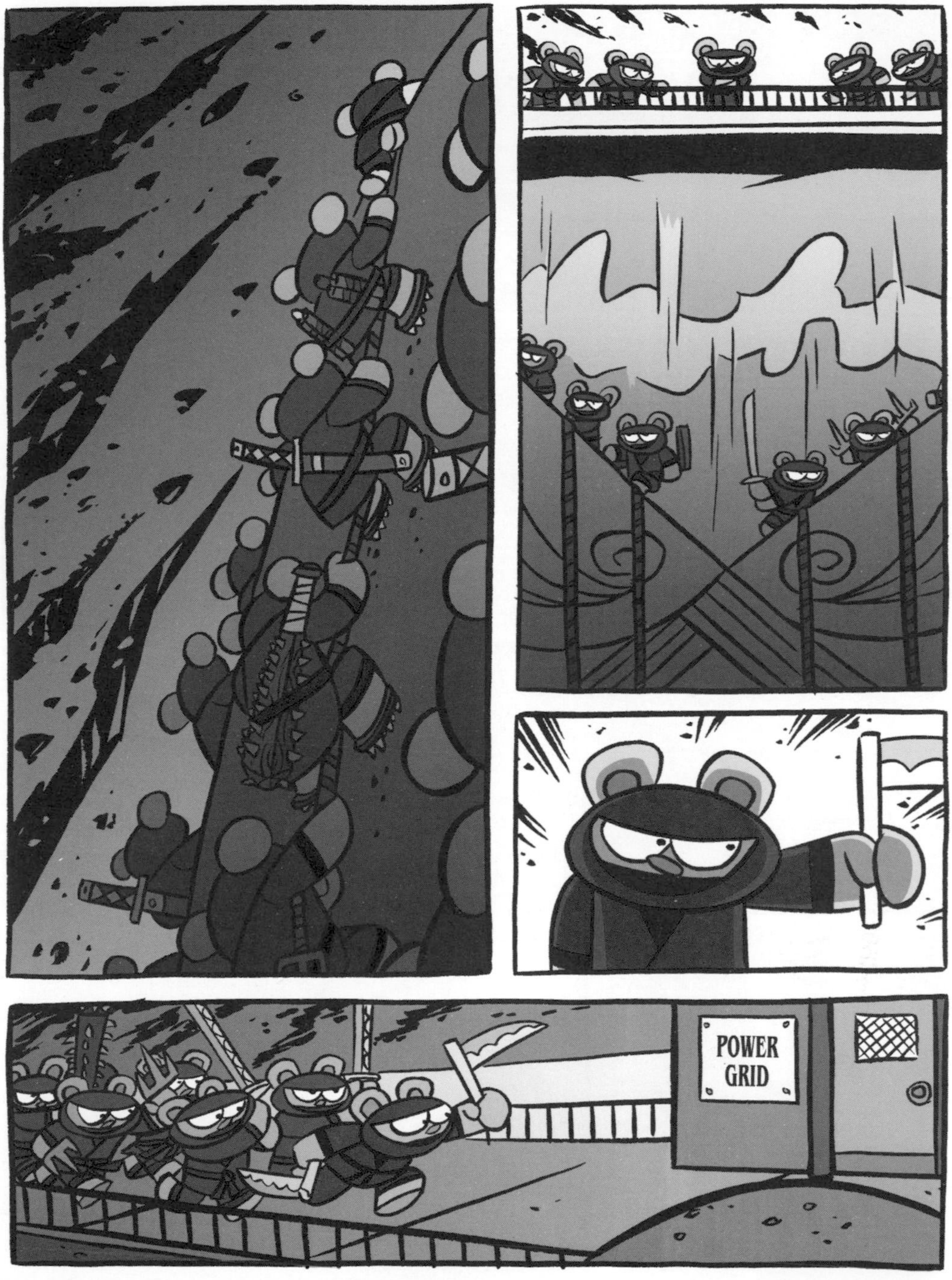
POWER
GRID

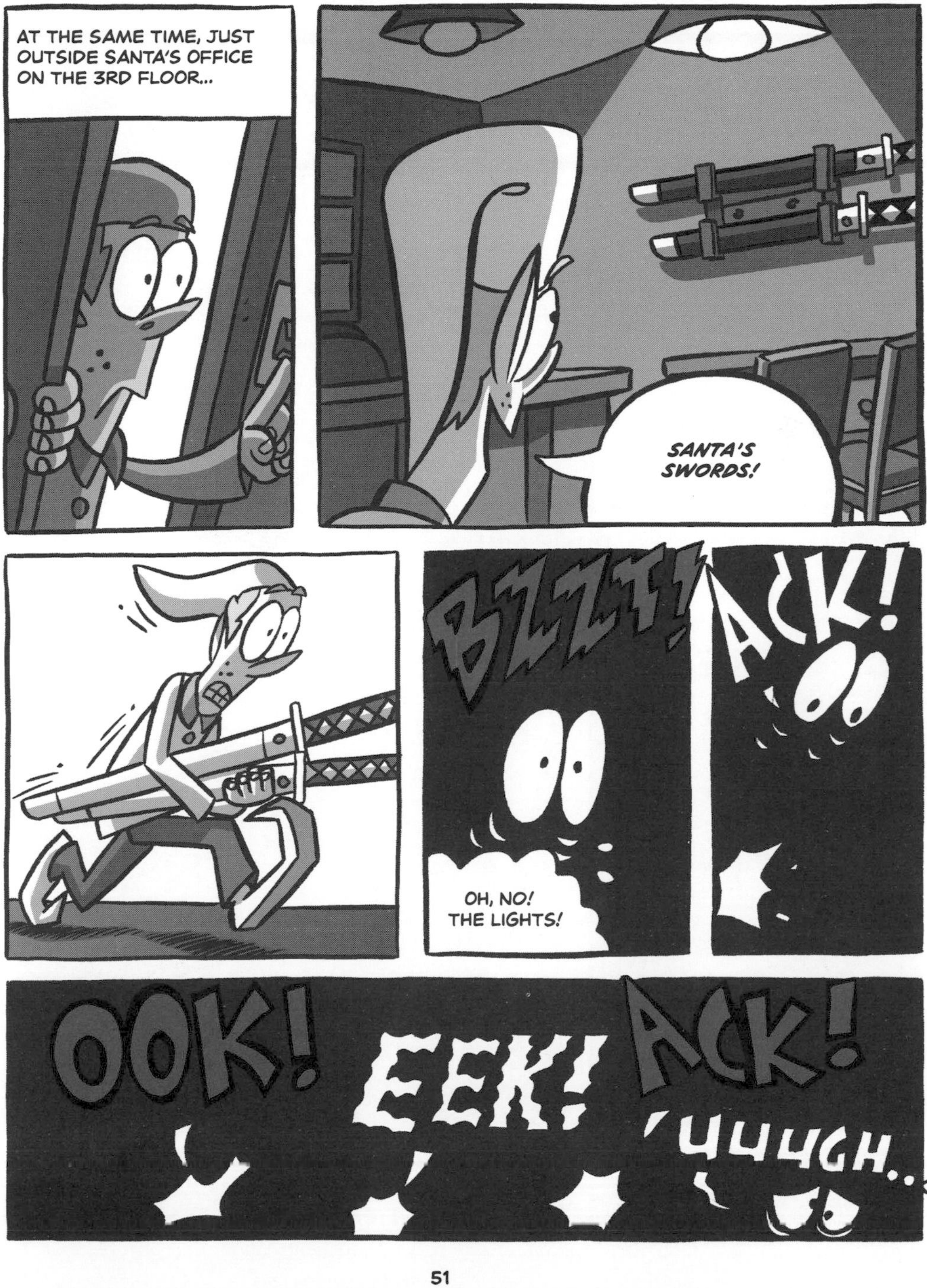
AT THE SAME TIME, JUST OUTSIDE SANTA'S OFFICE ON THE 3RD FLOOR...
SANTA'S SWORDS!
BZZT!
OH, NO! THE LIGHTS!
ACK!
OOK!
EEK!
ACK!
UUUGH...

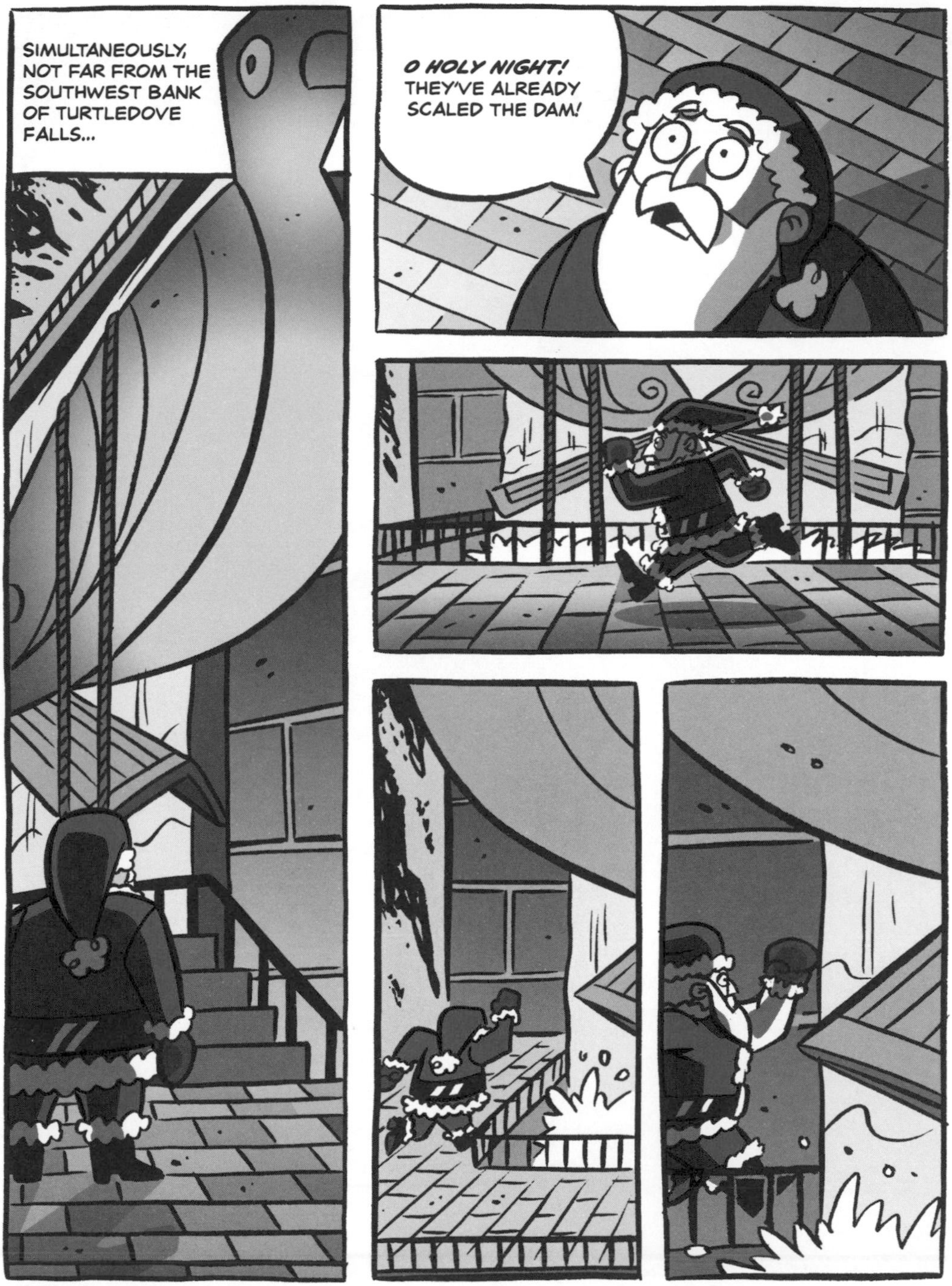
SIMULTANEOUSLY, NOT FAR FROM THE SOUTHWEST BANK OF TURTLEDOVE FALLS...
O HOLY NIGHT! THEY'VE ALREADY SCALED THE DAM!

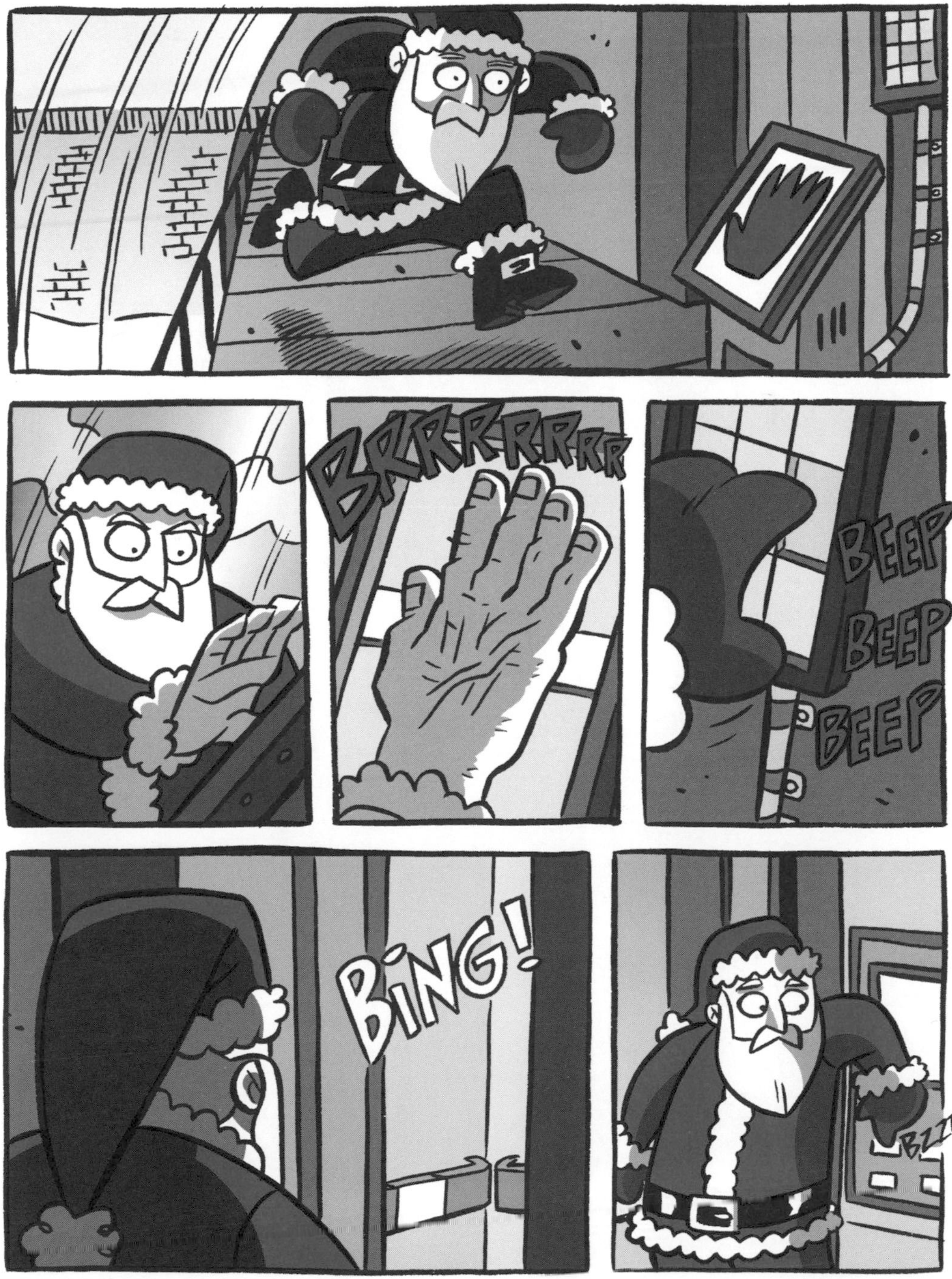
BRRRRRRRR
BEEP
BEEP
BEEP
BING!
BZZT!

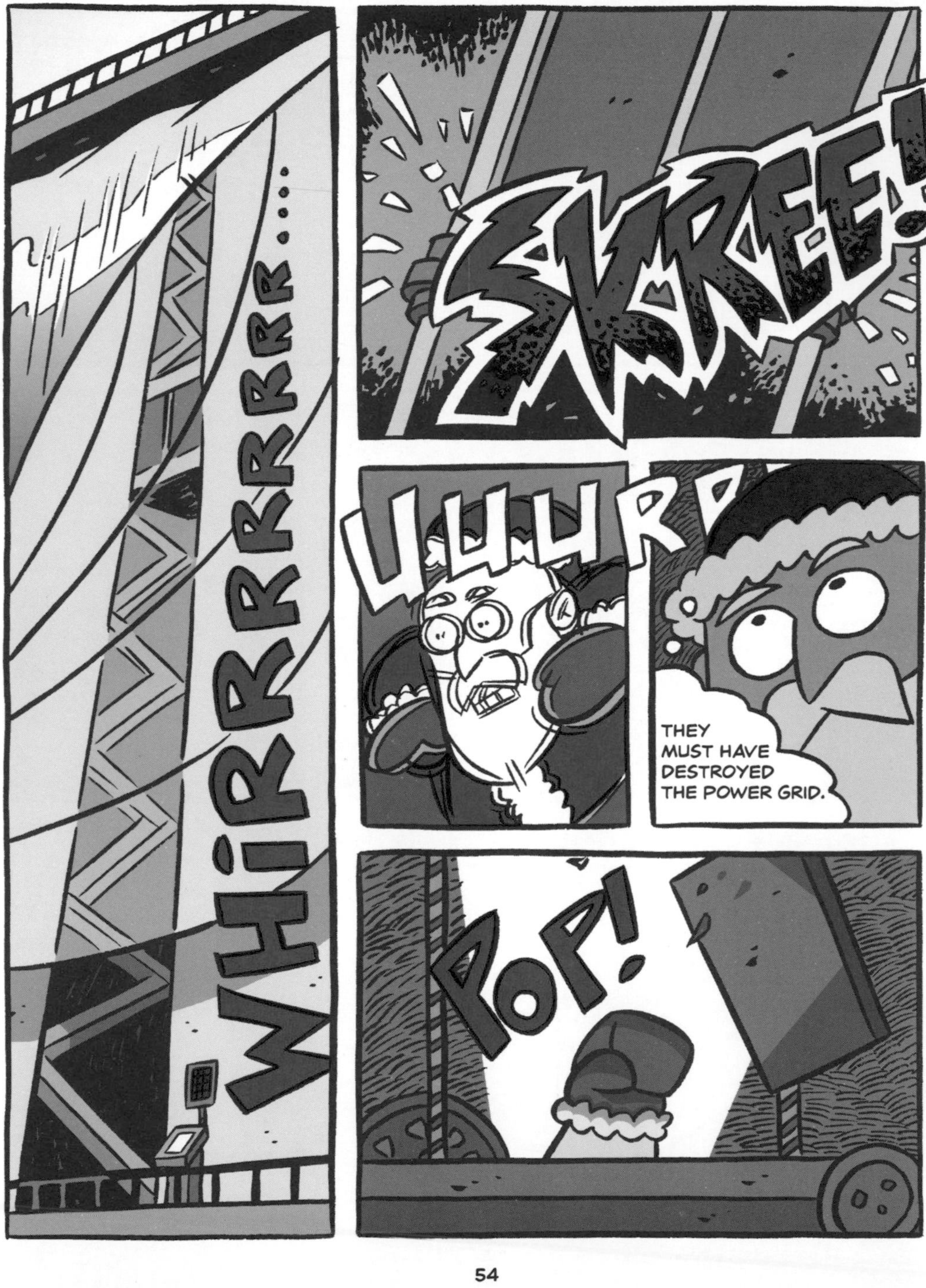
WHiRRRRRRR....
SKREE!
UUURD
THEY MUST HAVE DESTROYED THE POWER GRID.
POP!

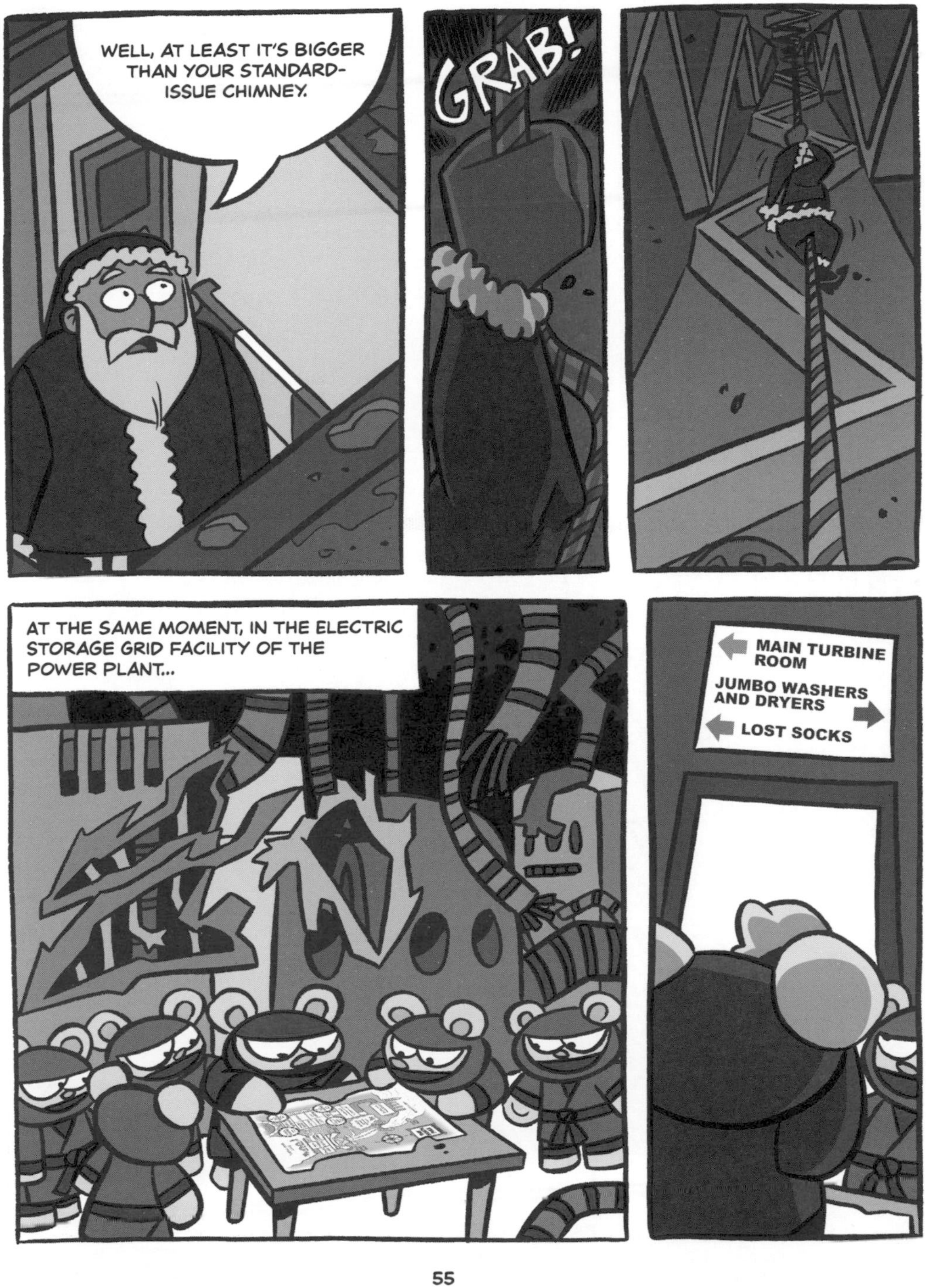

WELL, AT LEAST IT'S BIGGER THAN YOUR STANDARD-ISSUE CHIMNEY.
GRAB!
AT THE SAME MOMENT, IN THE ELECTRIC STORAGE GRID FACILITY OF THE POWER PLANT...
MAIN TURBINE ROOM
JUMBO WASHERS AND DRYERS
LOST SOCKS

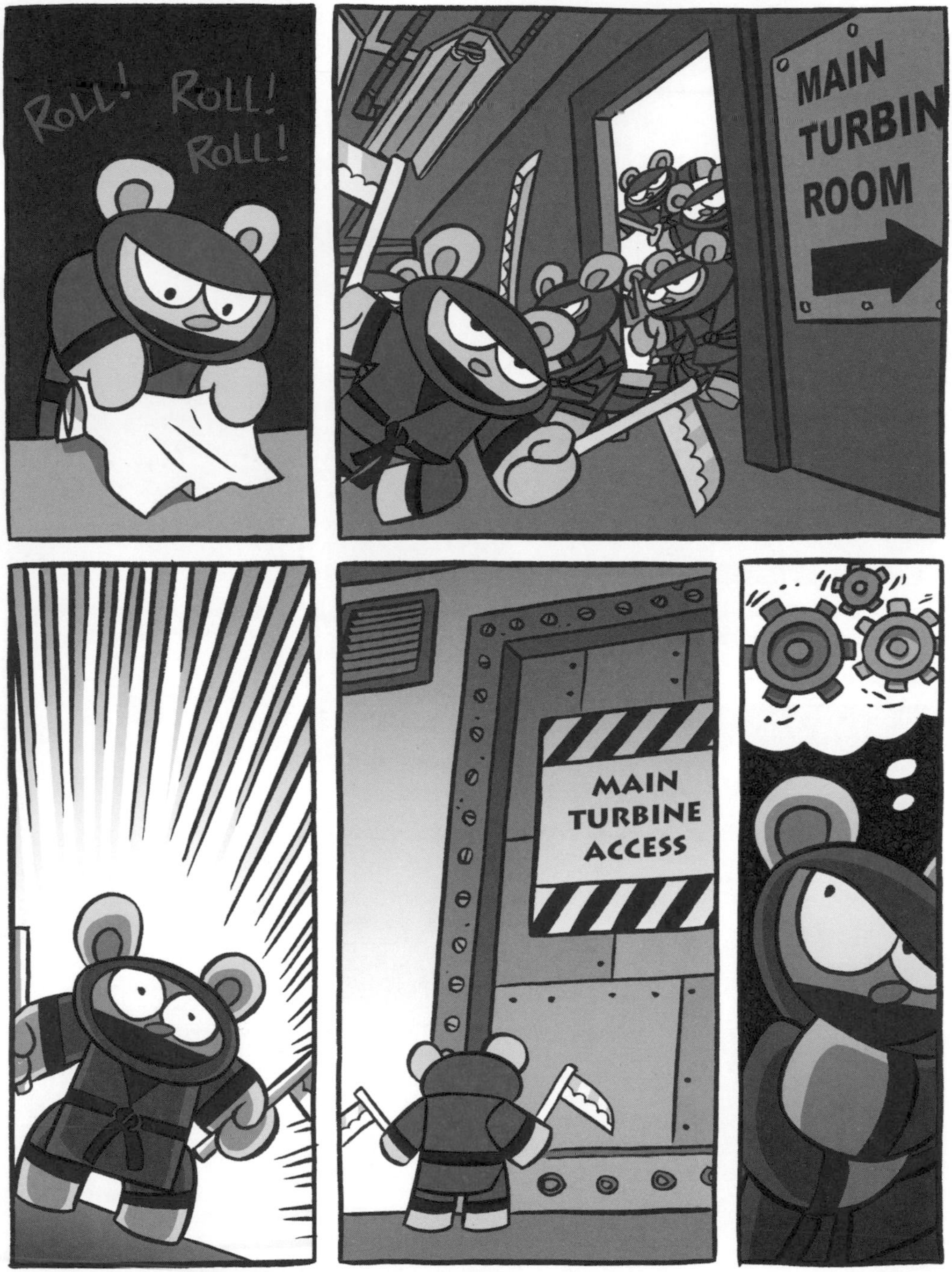
ROLL! ROLL!
ROLL!
MAIN
TURBIN
ROOM
MAIN
TURBINE
ACCESS

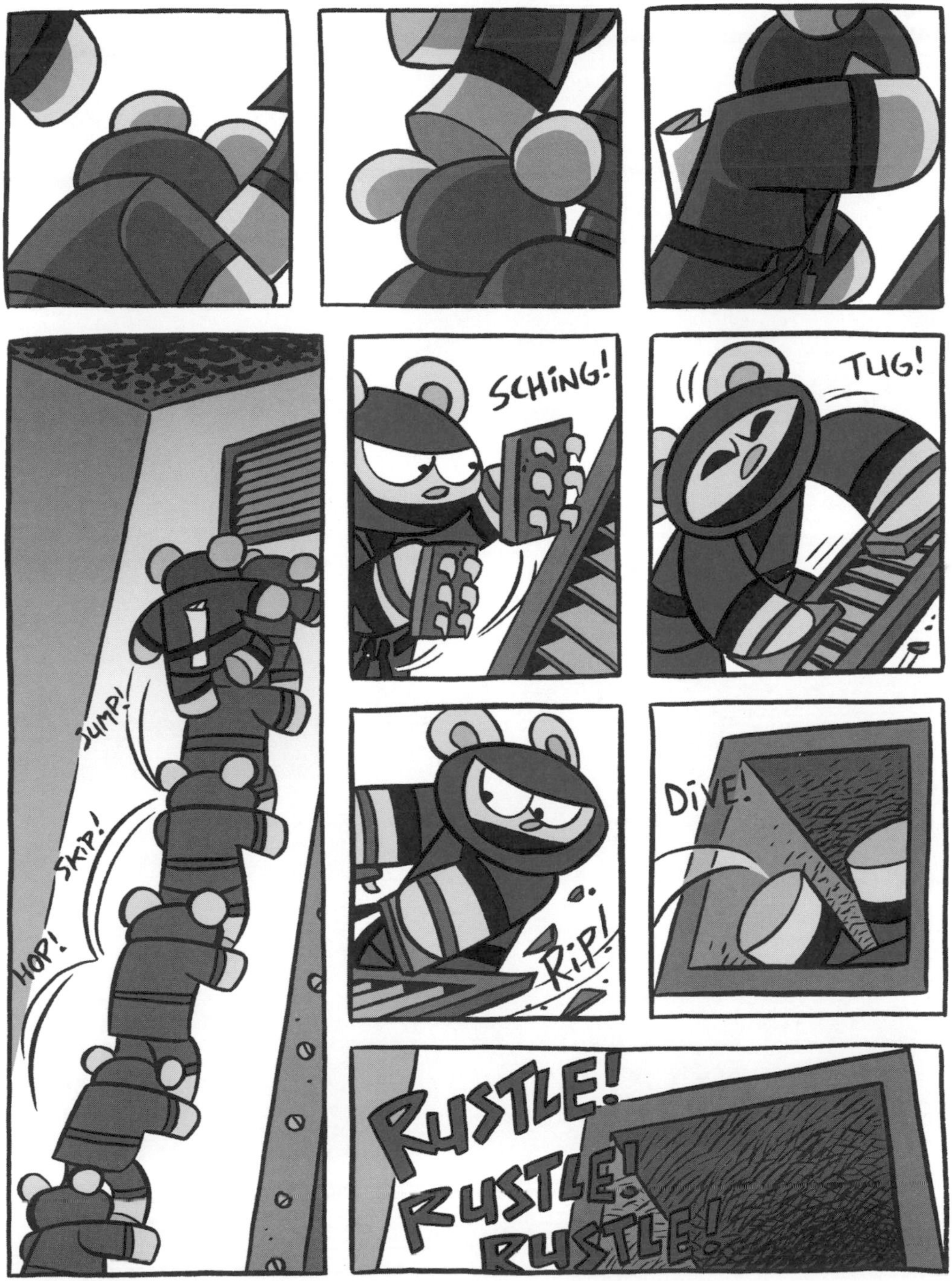

HOP!
SKIP!
JUMP!
SCHING!
TUG!
RIP!
DIVE!
RUSTLE!
RUSTLE!
RUSTLE!

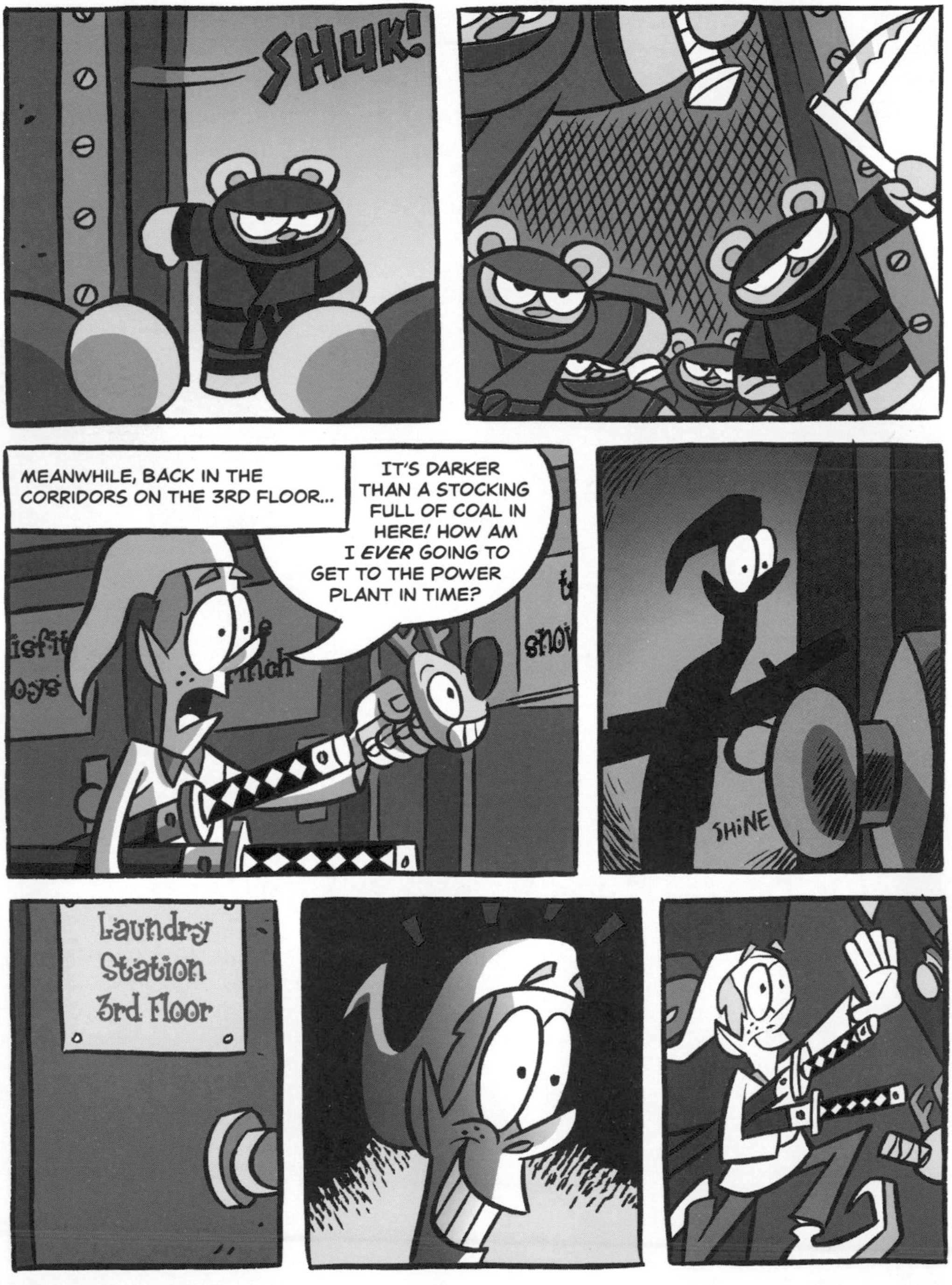
SHUK!
MEANWHILE, BACK IN THE CORRIDORS ON THE 3RD FLOOR...
IT'S DARKER THAN A STOCKING FULL OF COAL IN HERE! HOW AM I *EVER* GOING TO GET TO THE POWER PLANT IN TIME?
SHINE
Laundry Station 3rd Floor

SQUEAK! SQUEAK!

JUMP!

ELF KNICKERS

TURTLE DOVE DAM

ELF KNICKERS

SQUEAK! SQUEAK!

EEEEEEEEEE

ELF KNICKERS

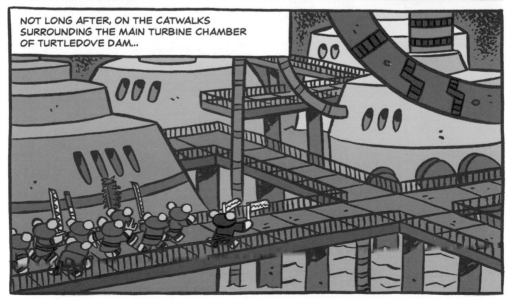

NOT LONG AFTER, ON THE CATWALKS SURROUNDING THE MAIN TURBINE CHAMBER OF TURTLEDOVE DAM...

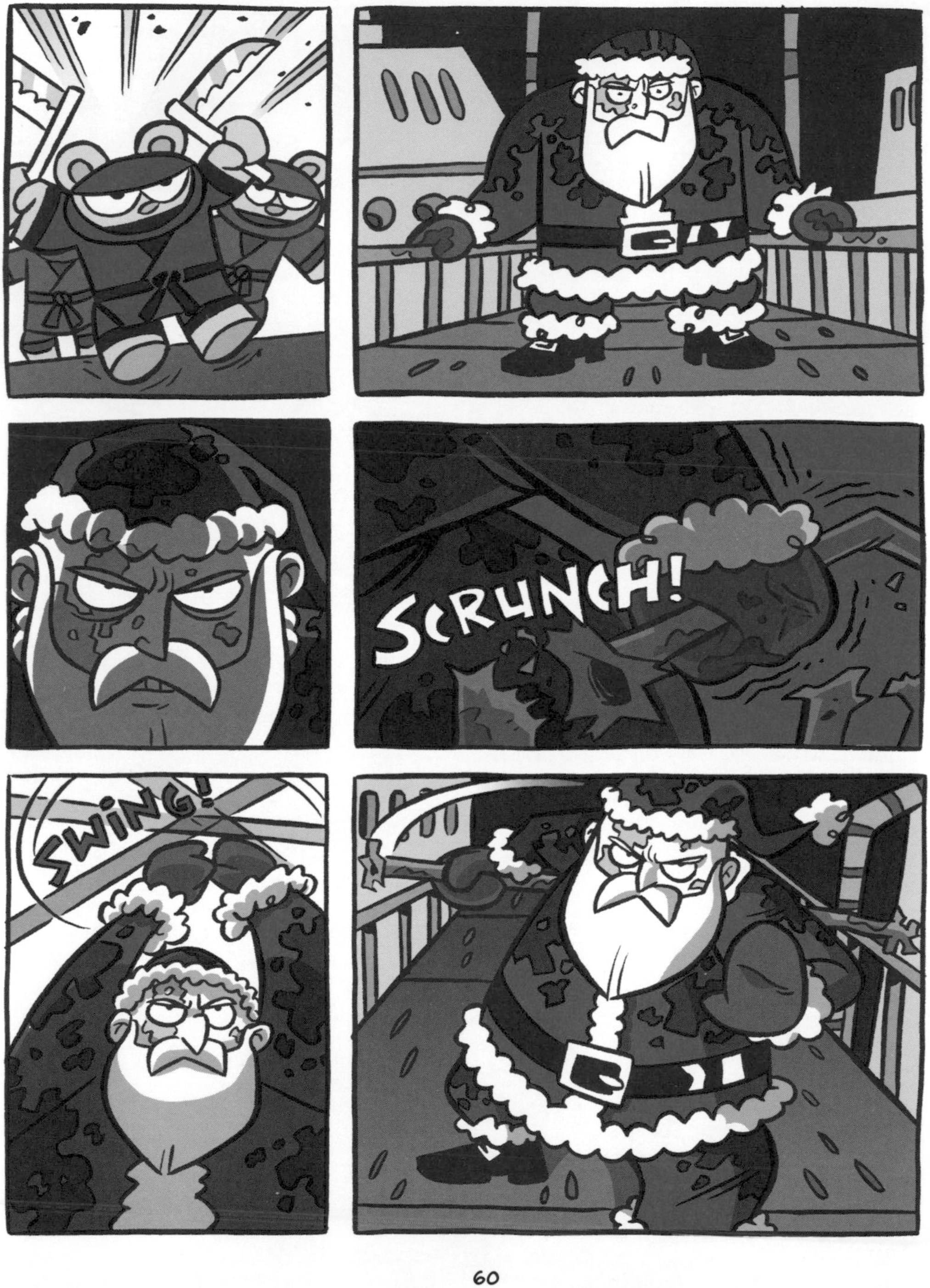
SCRUNCH!
SWING!

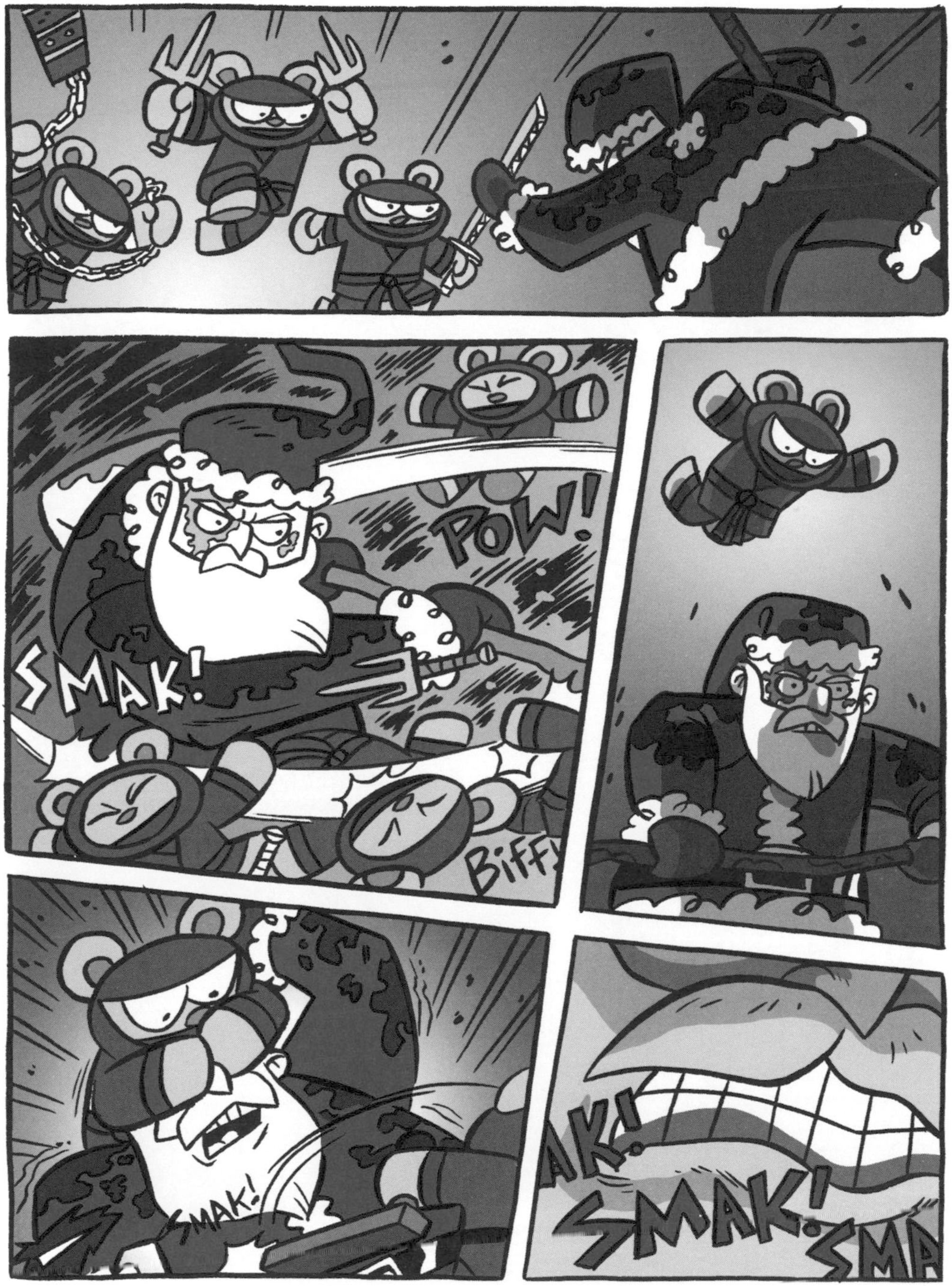
POW!
SMAK!
BIFF!
SMAK!
AK!
SMAK!
SMA

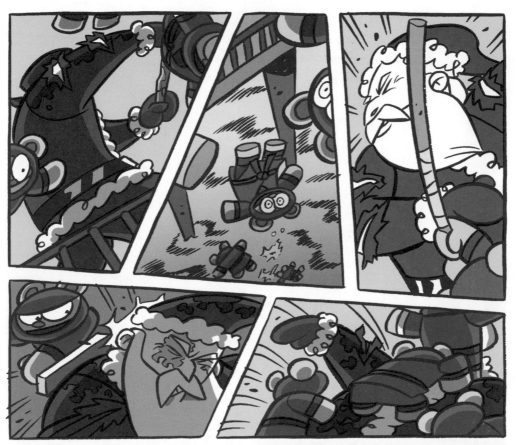

SECONDS LATER, IN THE MAIN RECEIVING ROOM OF THE WORKSHOP'S CENTRAL LAUNDRY FACILITY...

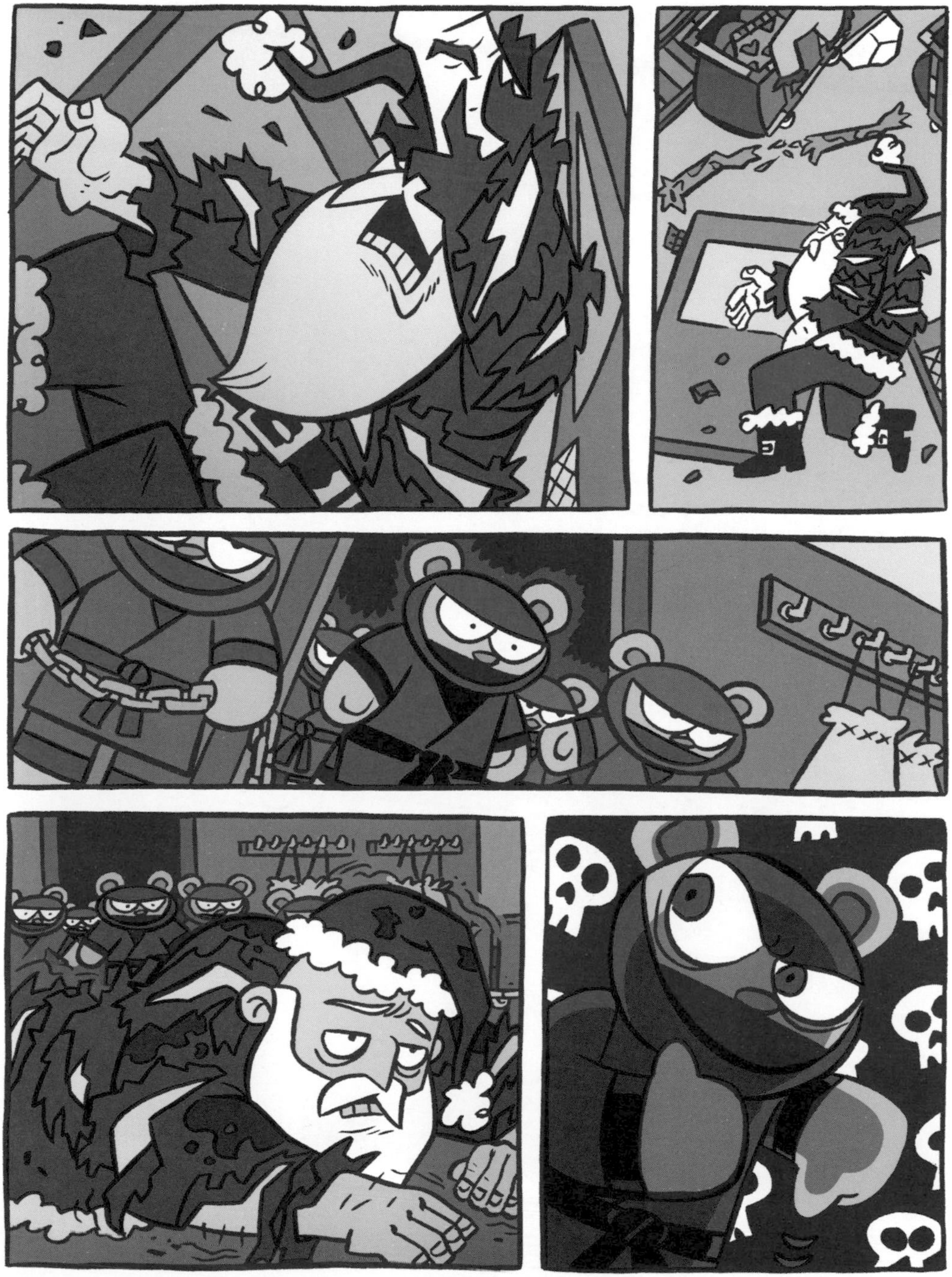

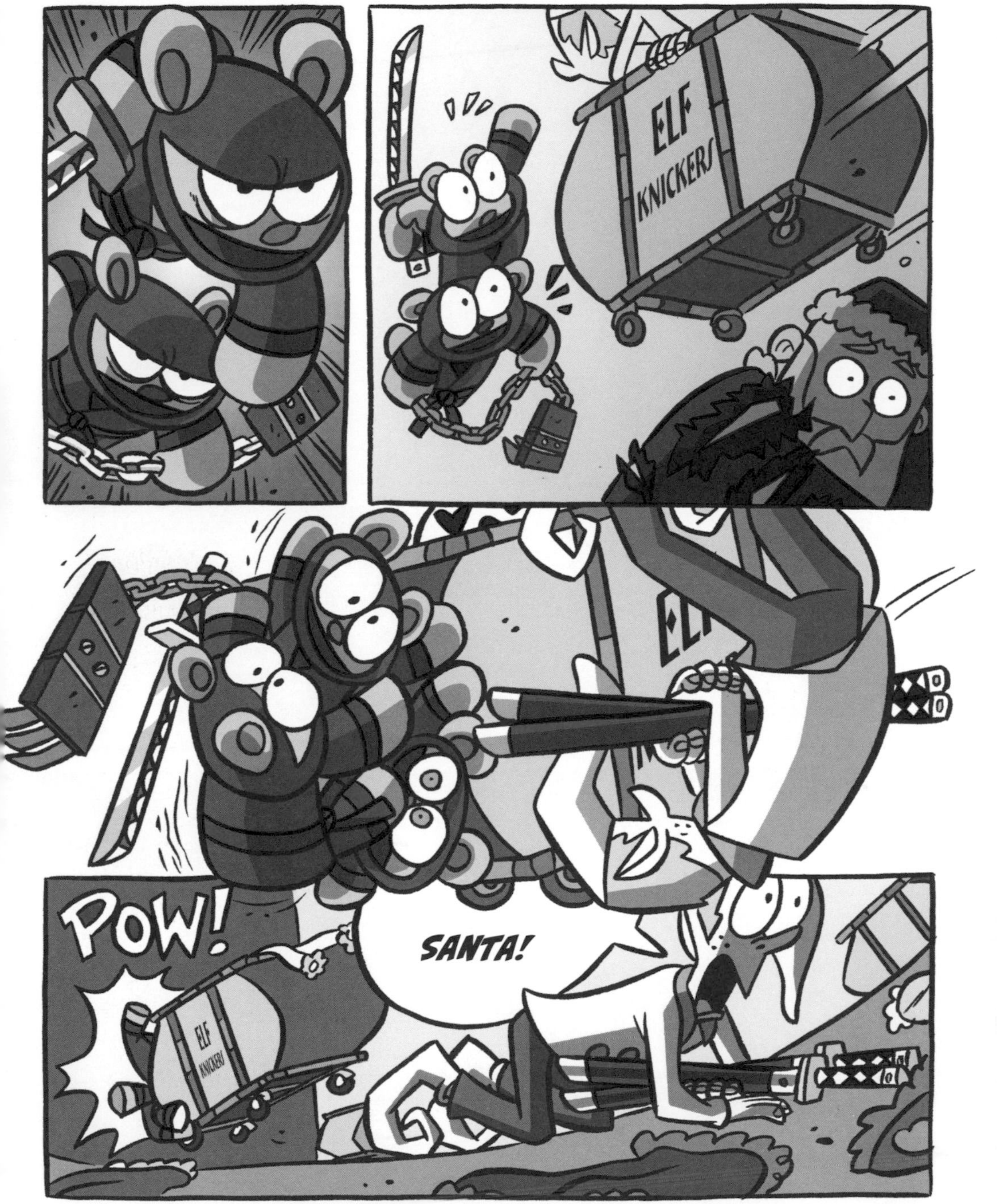
ELF KNICKERS
ELF
POW!
SANTA!
ELF KNICKERS

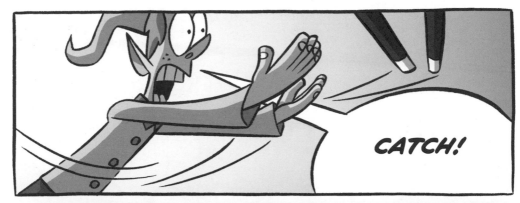

CATCH!

GRAB!

RIP!

TEAR!

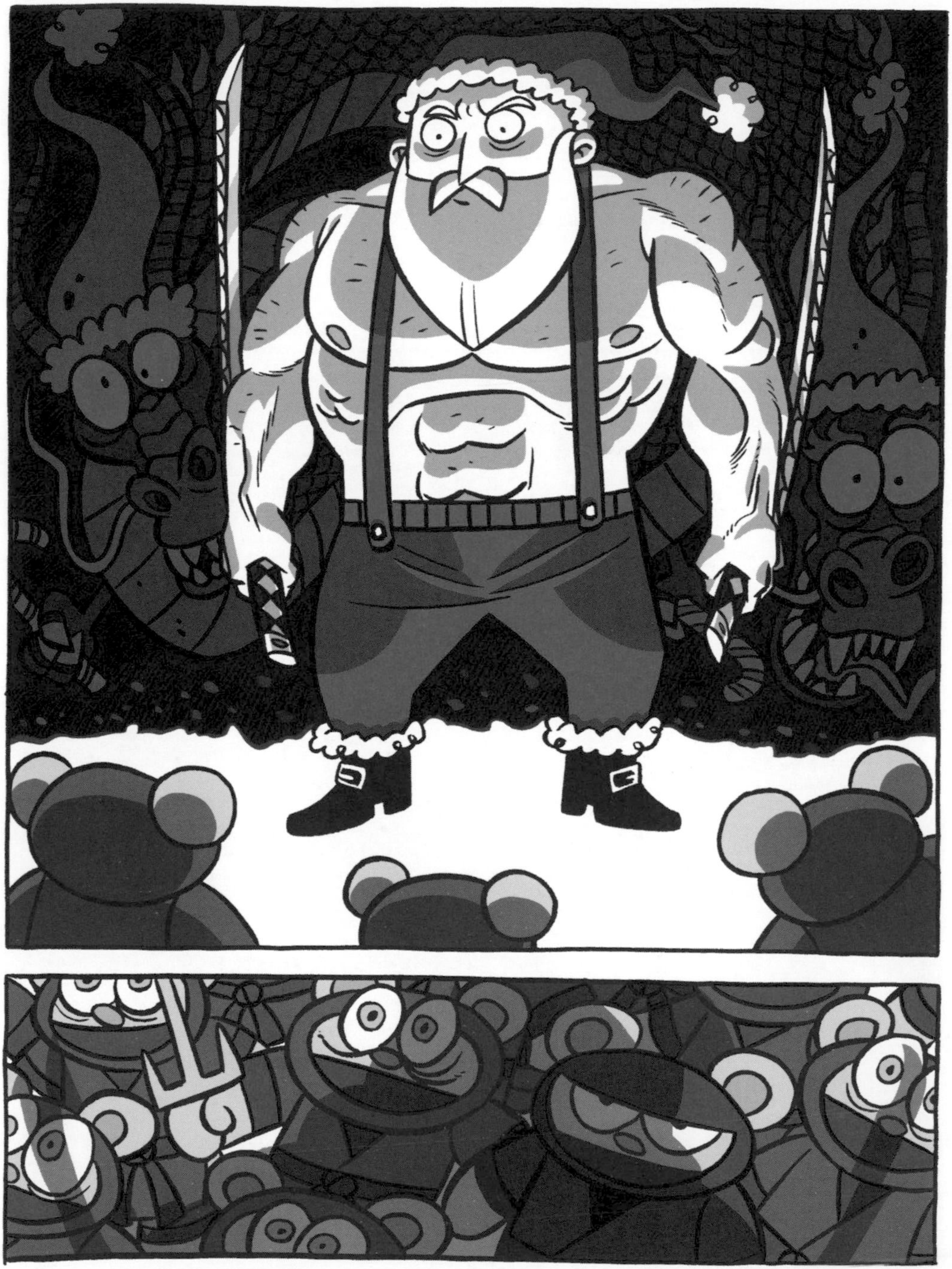

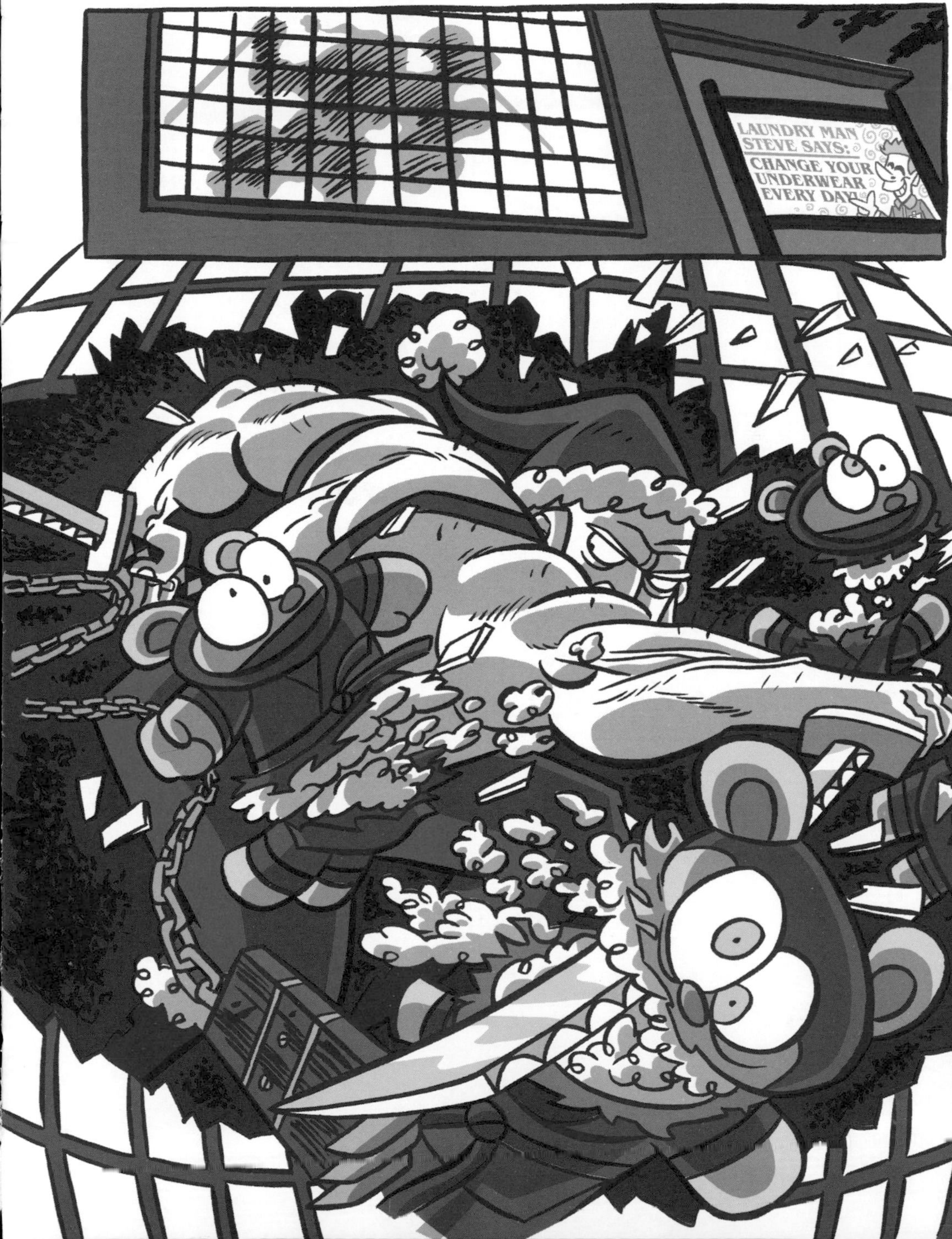
LAUNDRY MAN STEVE SAYS:
CHANGE YOUR UNDERWEAR EVERY DAY!

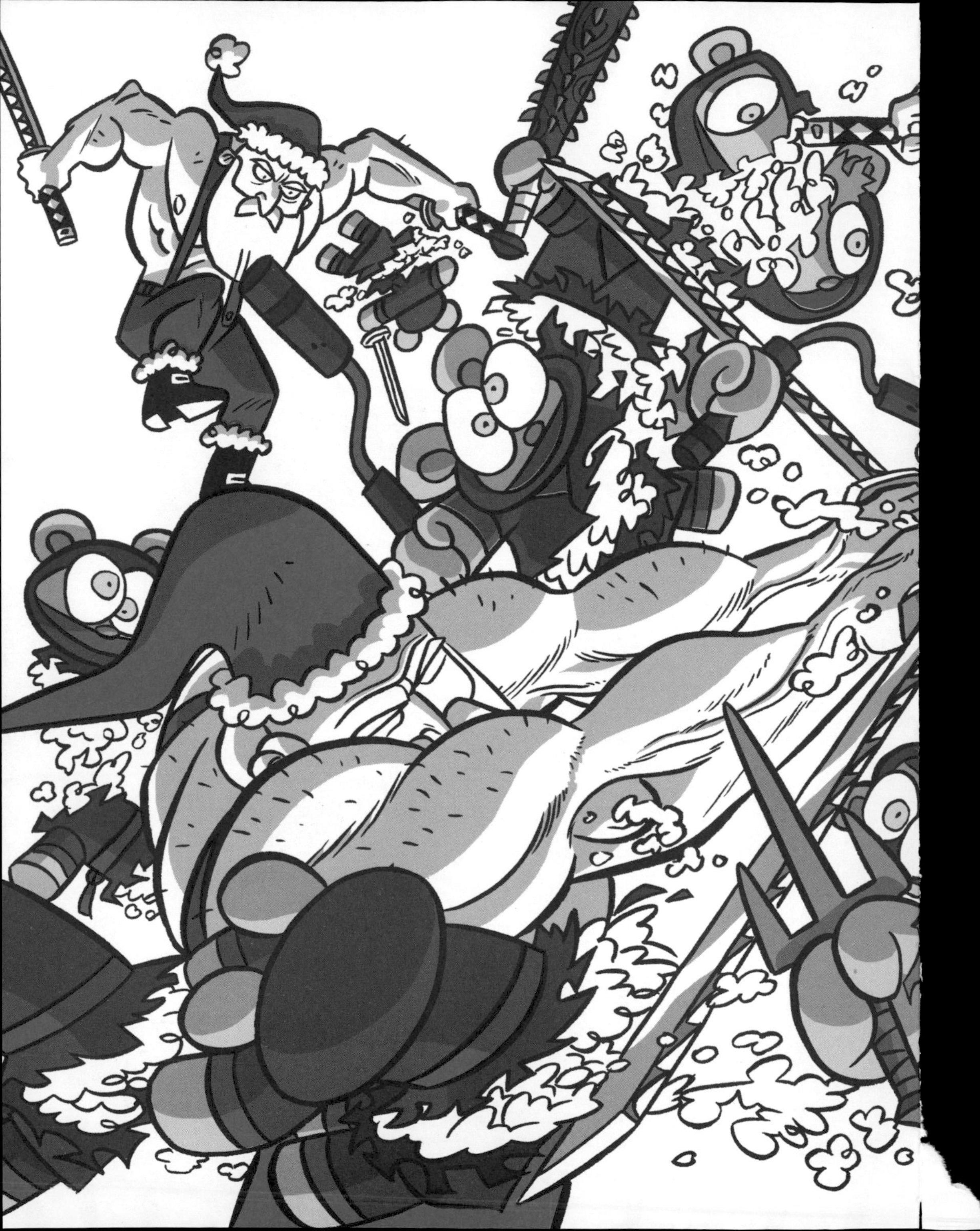

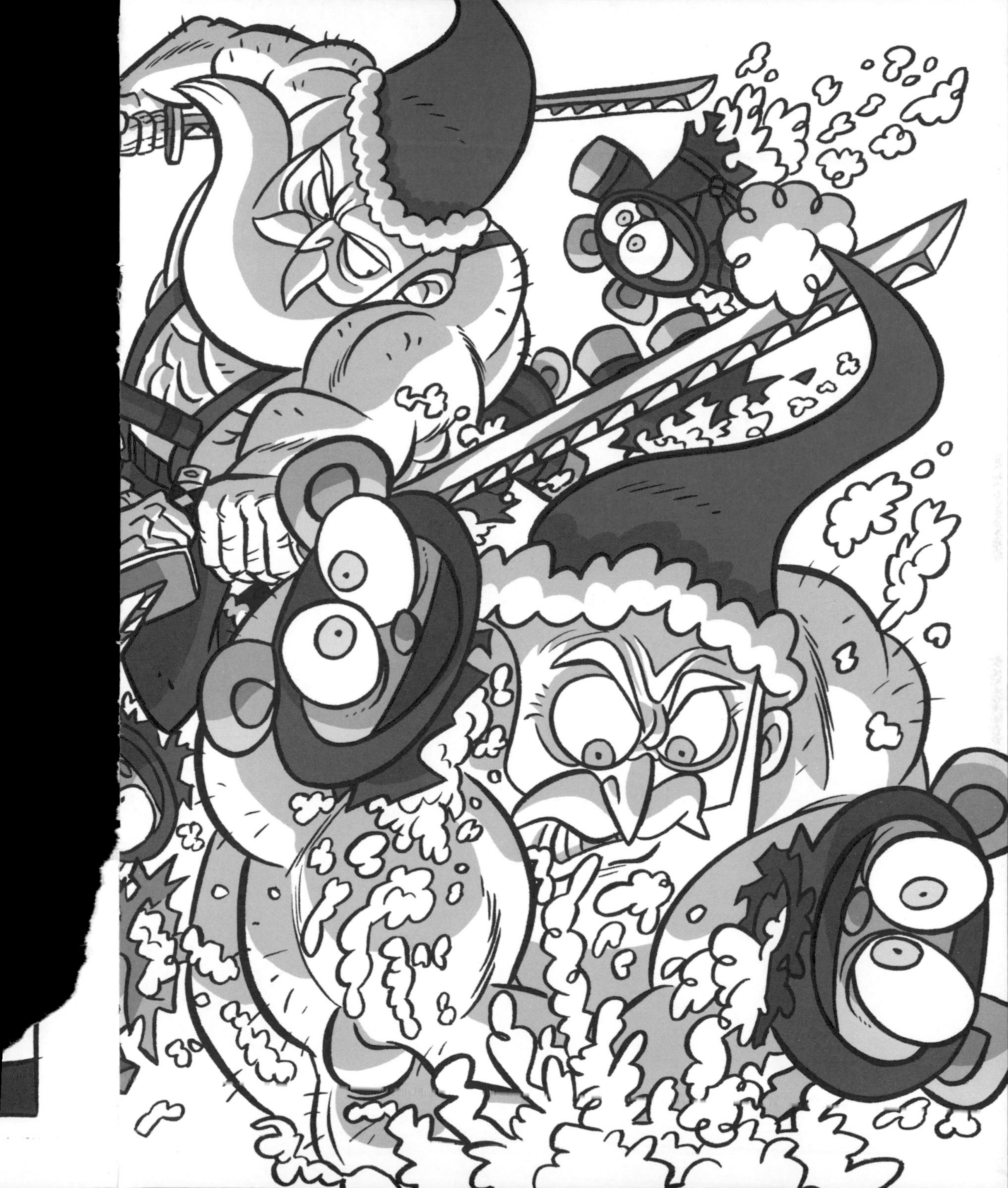

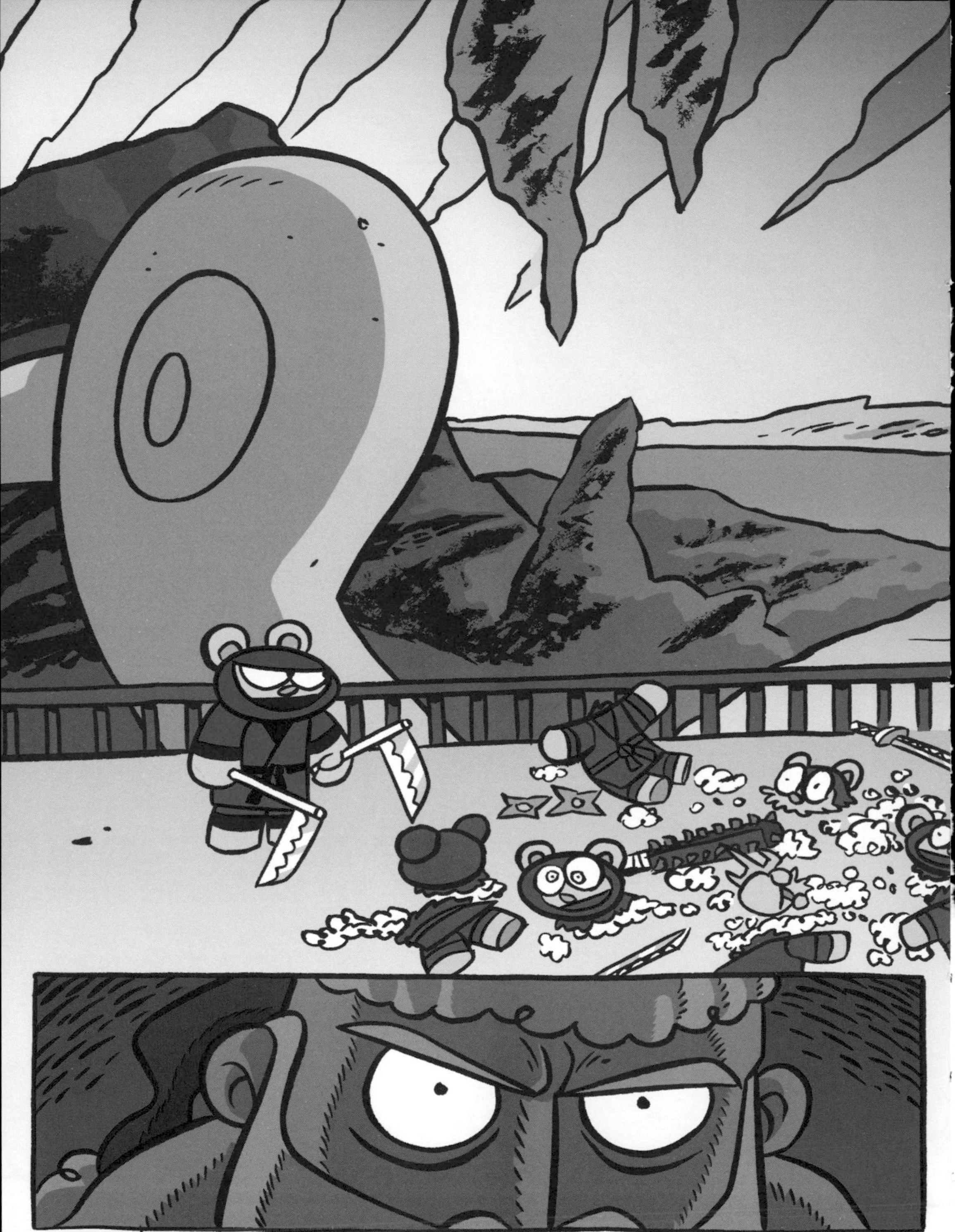

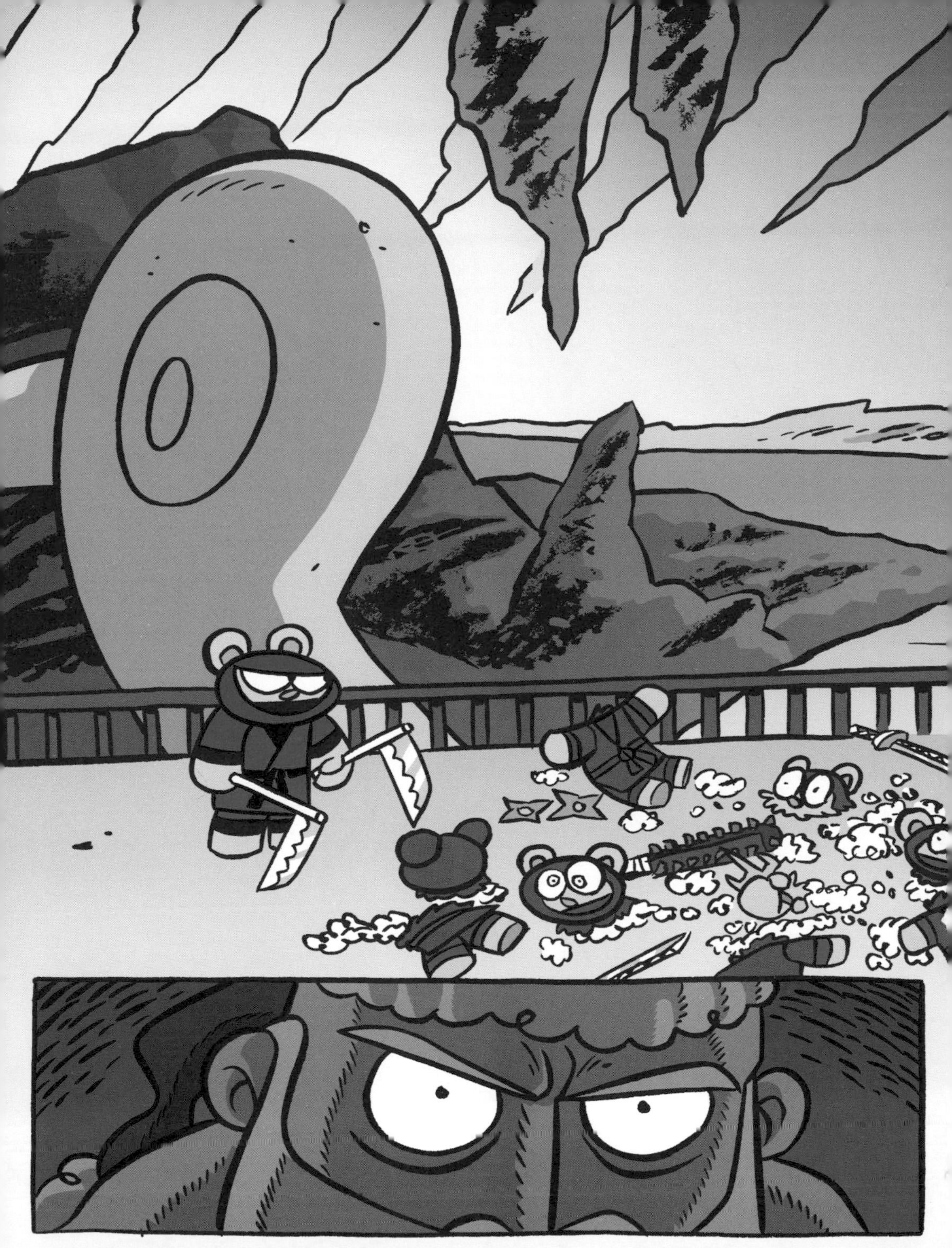

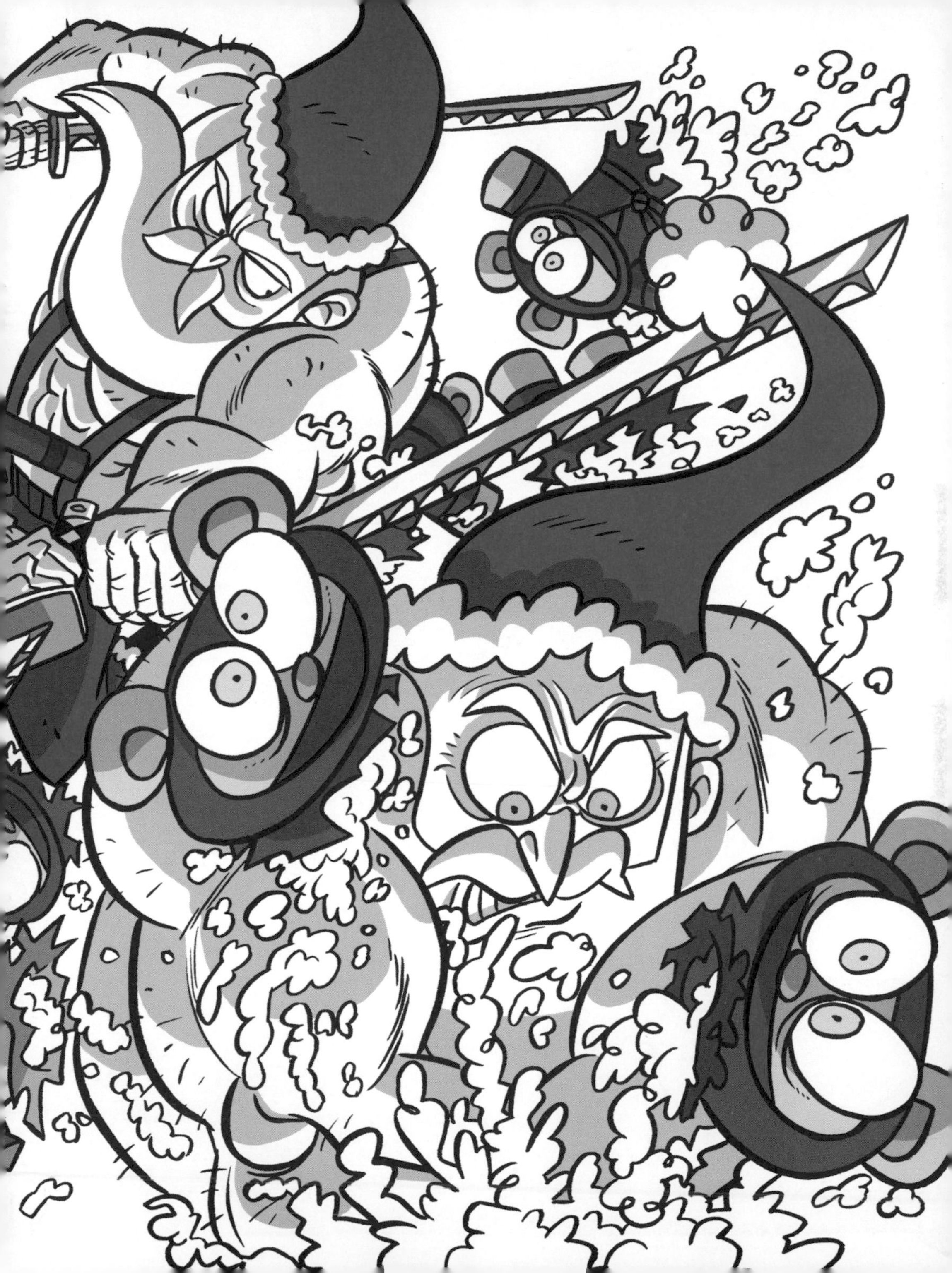

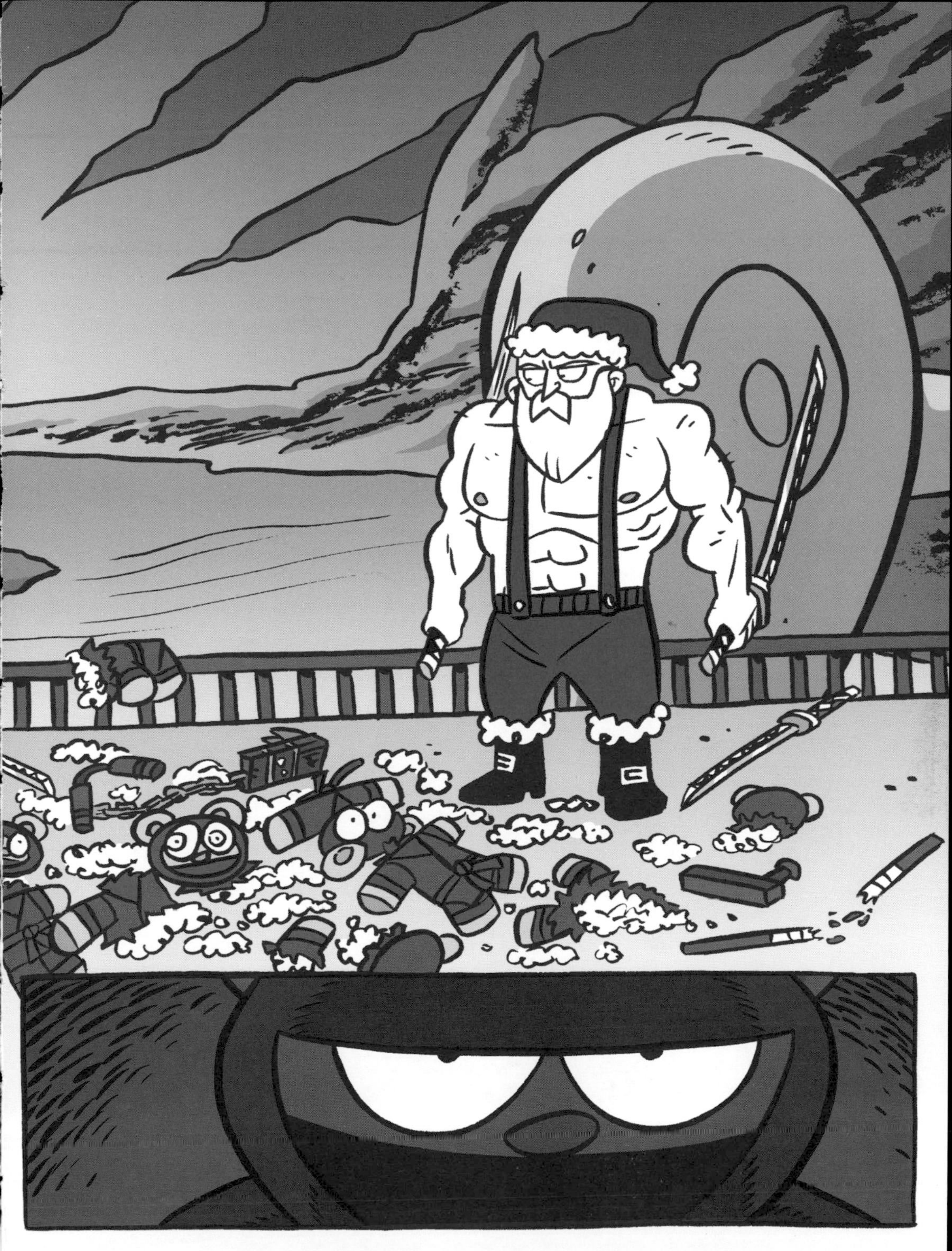

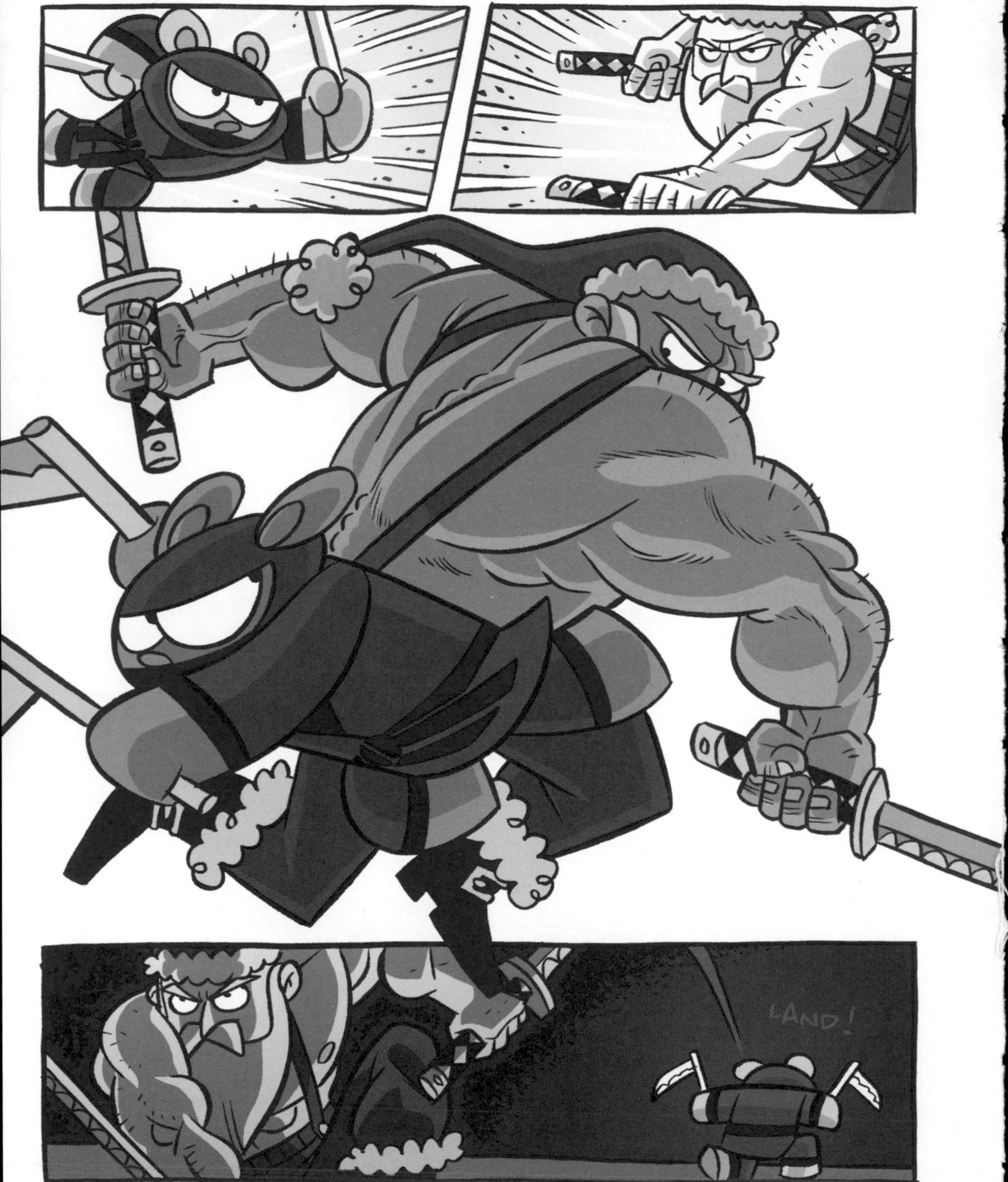
LAND!

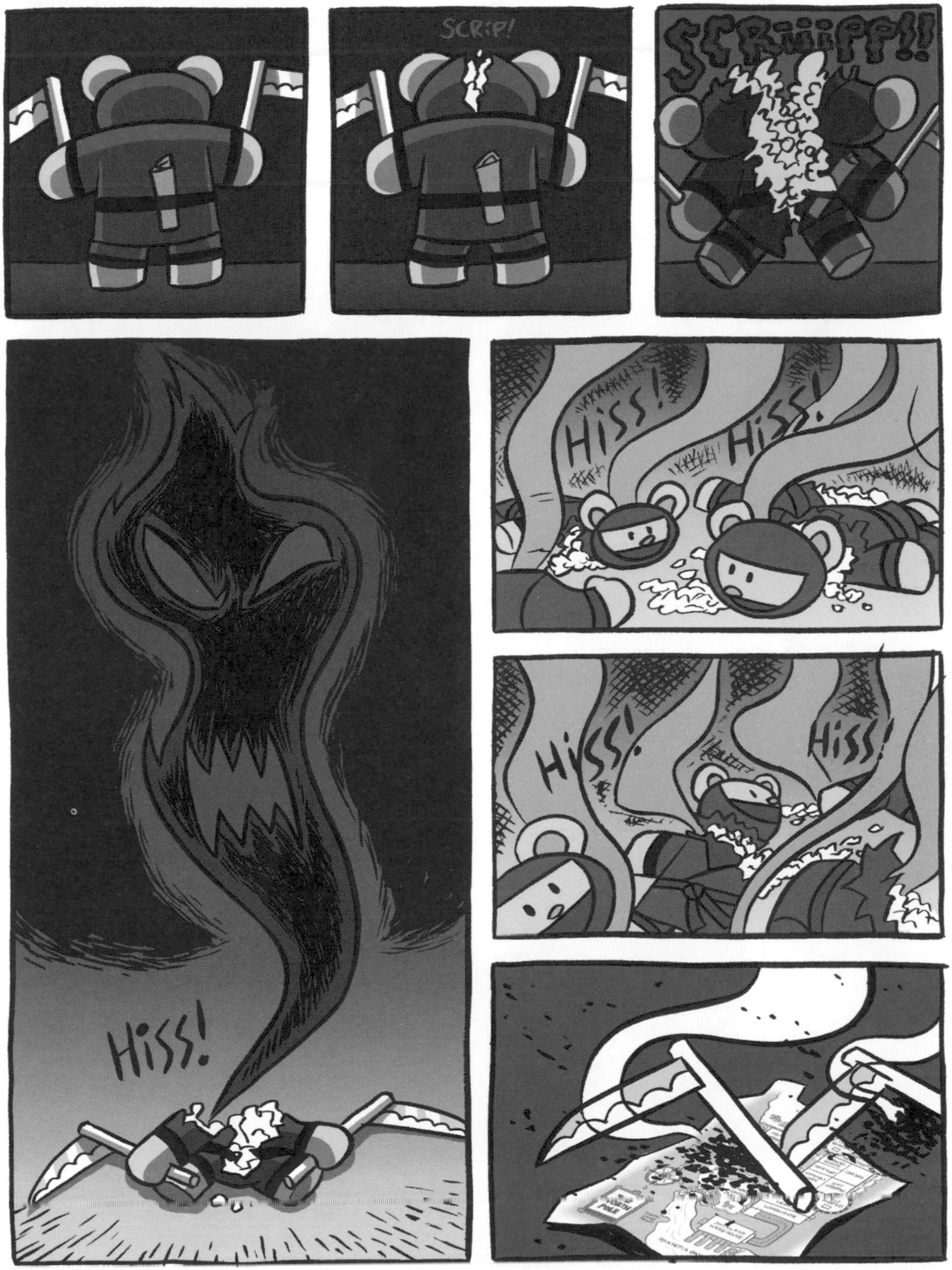
SCRiP!
SCRiiiPP!!
HiSS!
HiSS!
HiSS!
HiSS!
HiSS!

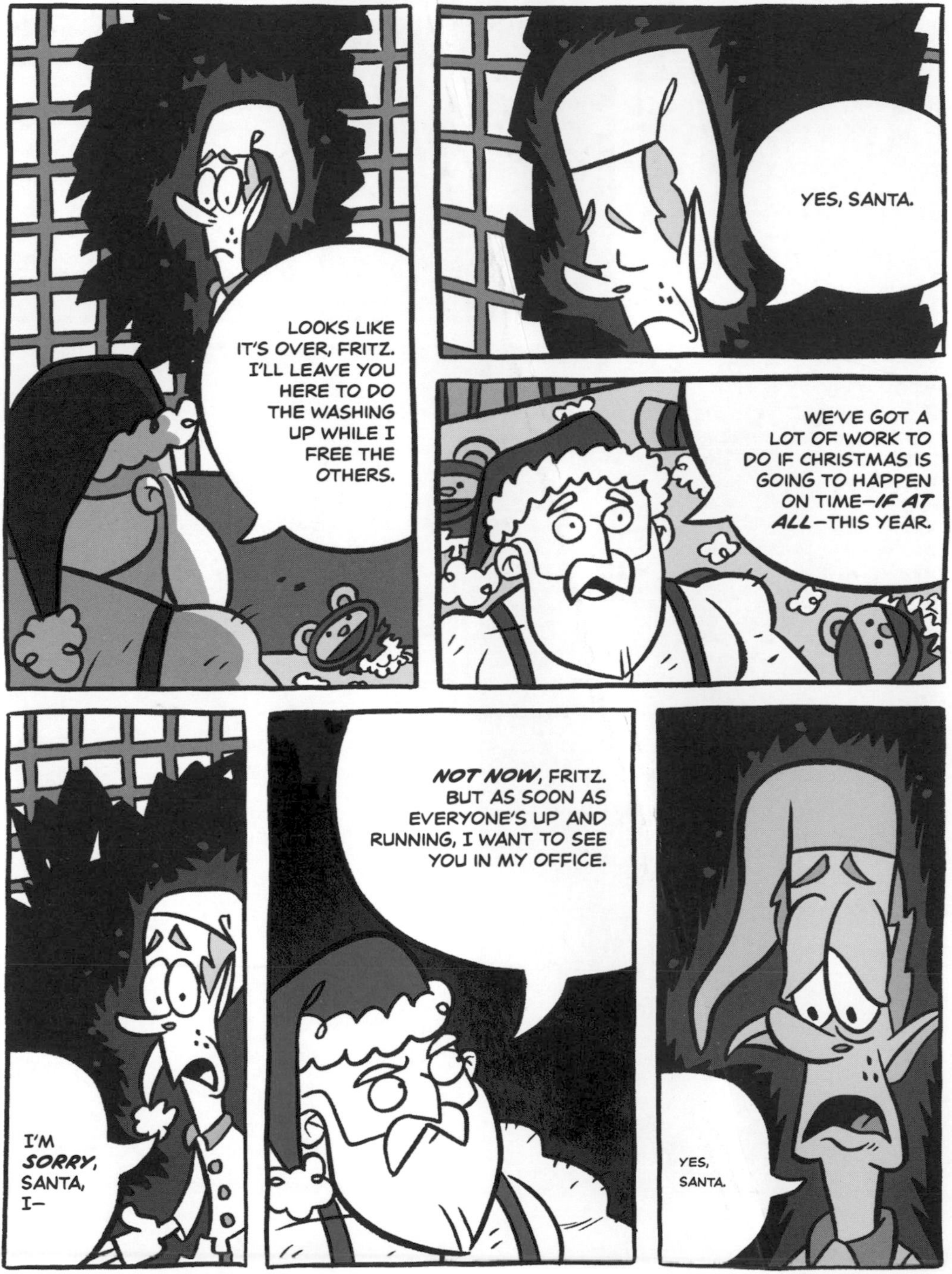
LOOKS LIKE IT'S OVER, FRITZ. I'LL LEAVE YOU HERE TO DO THE WASHING UP WHILE I FREE THE OTHERS.
YES, SANTA.
WE'VE GOT A LOT OF WORK TO DO IF CHRISTMAS IS GOING TO HAPPEN ON TIME—*IF AT ALL*—THIS YEAR.
I'M *SORRY*, SANTA, I—
NOT NOW, FRITZ. BUT AS SOON AS EVERYONE'S UP AND RUNNING, I WANT TO SEE YOU IN MY OFFICE.
YES, SANTA.

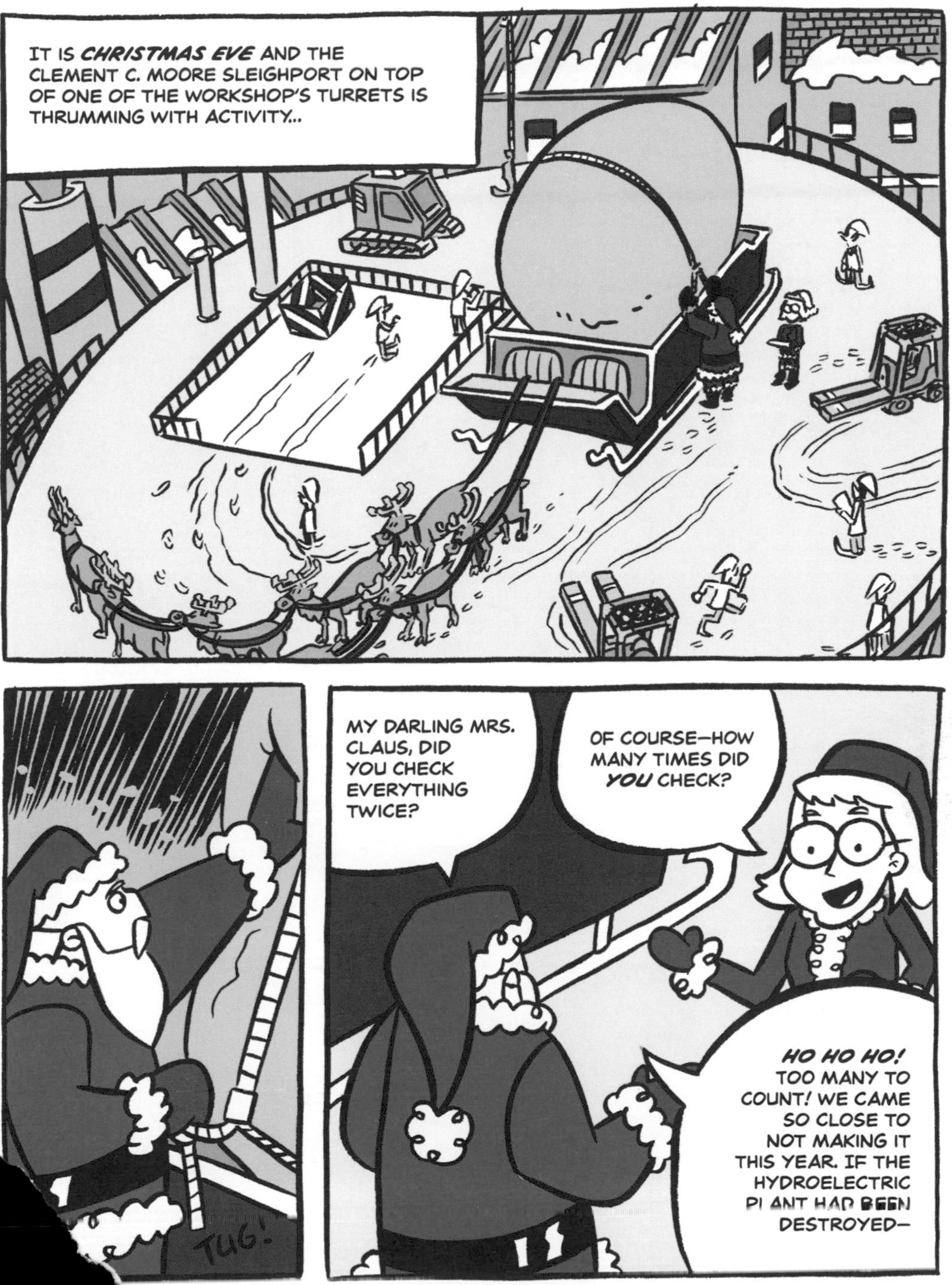
IT IS *CHRISTMAS EVE* AND THE CLEMENT C. MOORE SLEIGHPORT ON TOP OF ONE OF THE WORKSHOP'S TURRETS IS THRUMMING WITH ACTIVITY...
TUG!
MY DARLING MRS. CLAUS, DID YOU CHECK EVERYTHING TWICE?
OF COURSE—HOW MANY TIMES DID *YOU* CHECK?
HO HO HO! TOO MANY TO COUNT! WE CAME SO CLOSE TO NOT MAKING IT THIS YEAR. IF THE HYDROELECTRIC PLANT HAD BEEN DESTROYED—

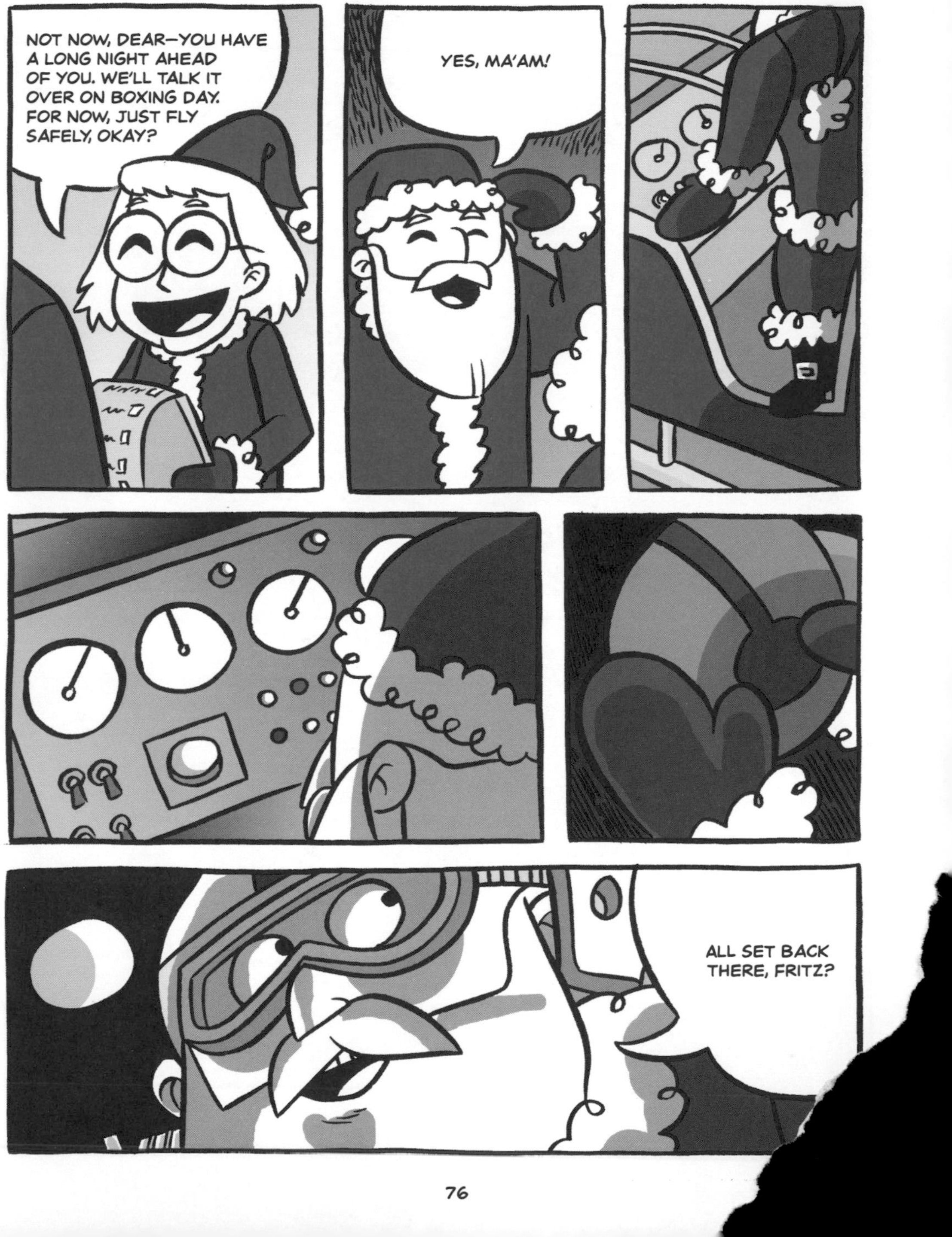
NOT NOW, DEAR—YOU HAVE A LONG NIGHT AHEAD OF YOU. WE'LL TALK IT OVER ON BOXING DAY. FOR NOW, JUST FLY SAFELY, OKAY?
YES, MA'AM!
ALL SET BACK THERE, FRITZ?

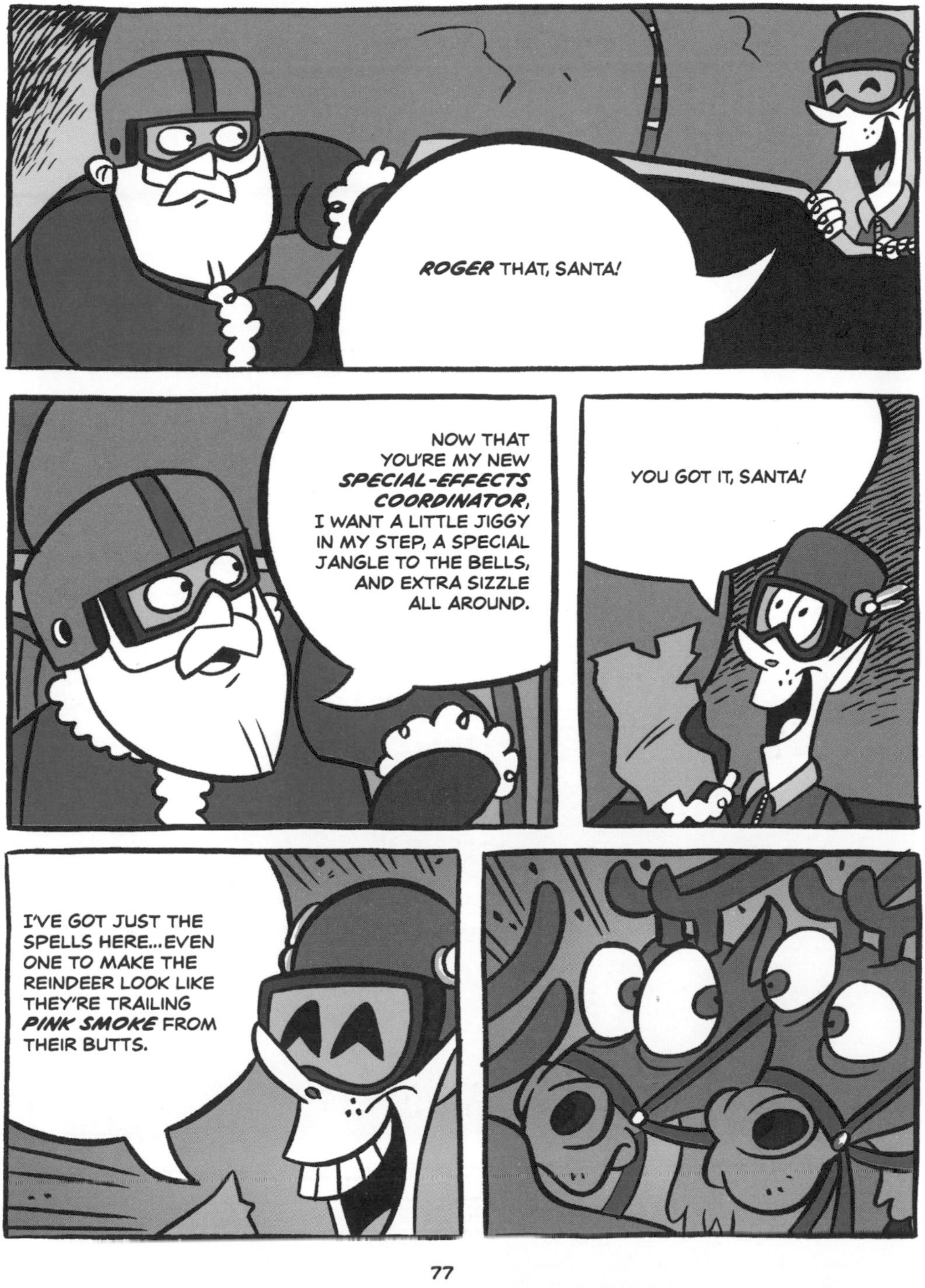
ROGER THAT, SANTA!
NOW THAT YOU'RE MY NEW SPECIAL-EFFECTS COORDINATOR, I WANT A LITTLE JIGGY IN MY STEP, A SPECIAL JANGLE TO THE BELLS, AND EXTRA SIZZLE ALL AROUND.
YOU GOT IT, SANTA!
I'VE GOT JUST THE SPELLS HERE...EVEN ONE TO MAKE THE REINDEER LOOK LIKE THEY'RE TRAILING PINK SMOKE FROM THEIR BUTTS.

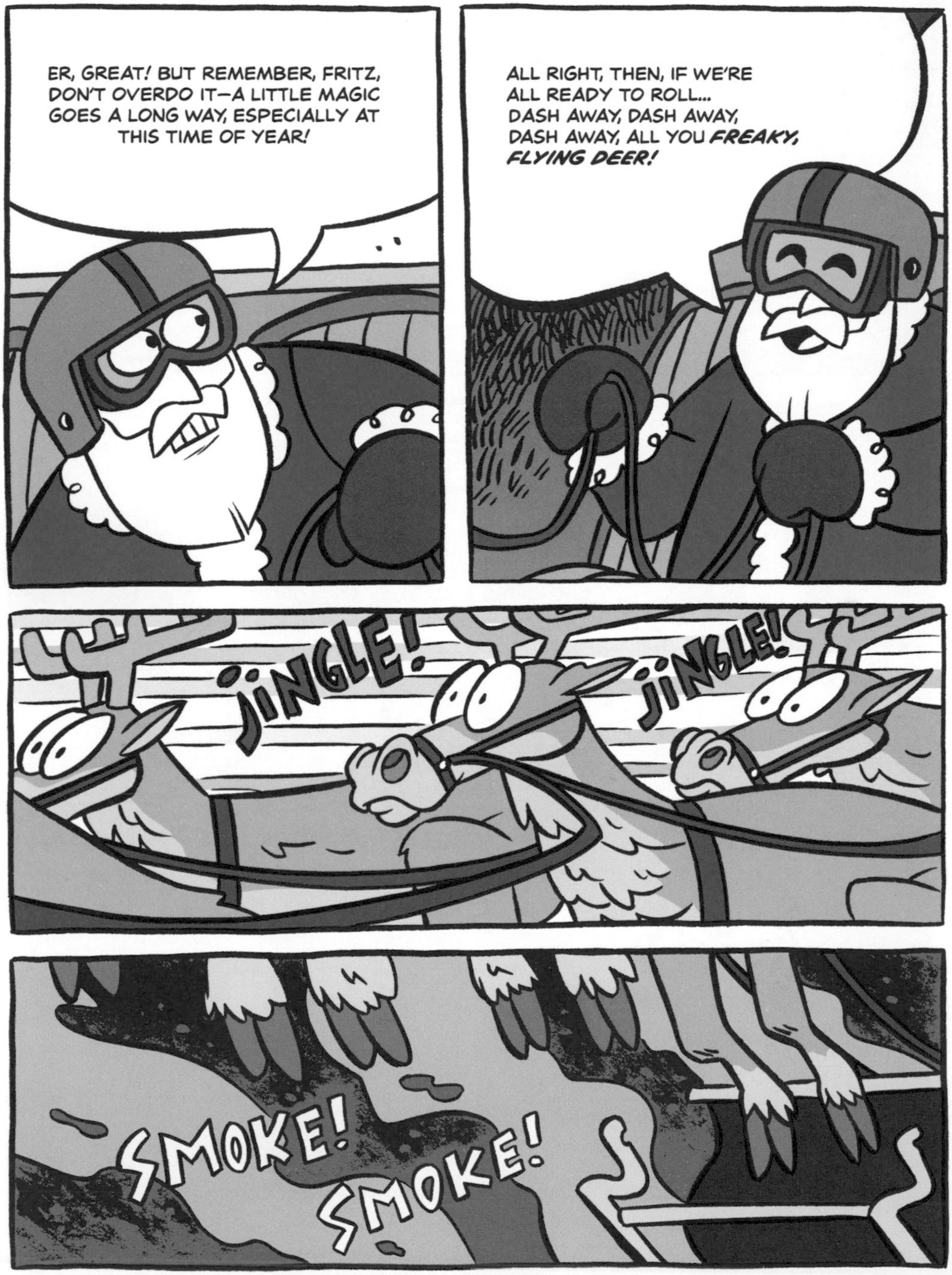
ER, GREAT! BUT REMEMBER, FRITZ, DON'T OVERDO IT—A LITTLE MAGIC GOES A LONG WAY, ESPECIALLY AT THIS TIME OF YEAR!
ALL RIGHT, THEN, IF WE'RE ALL READY TO ROLL... DASH AWAY, DASH AWAY, DASH AWAY, ALL YOU *FREAKY, FLYING DEER!*
JINGLE!
JINGLE!
SMOKE!
SMOKE!

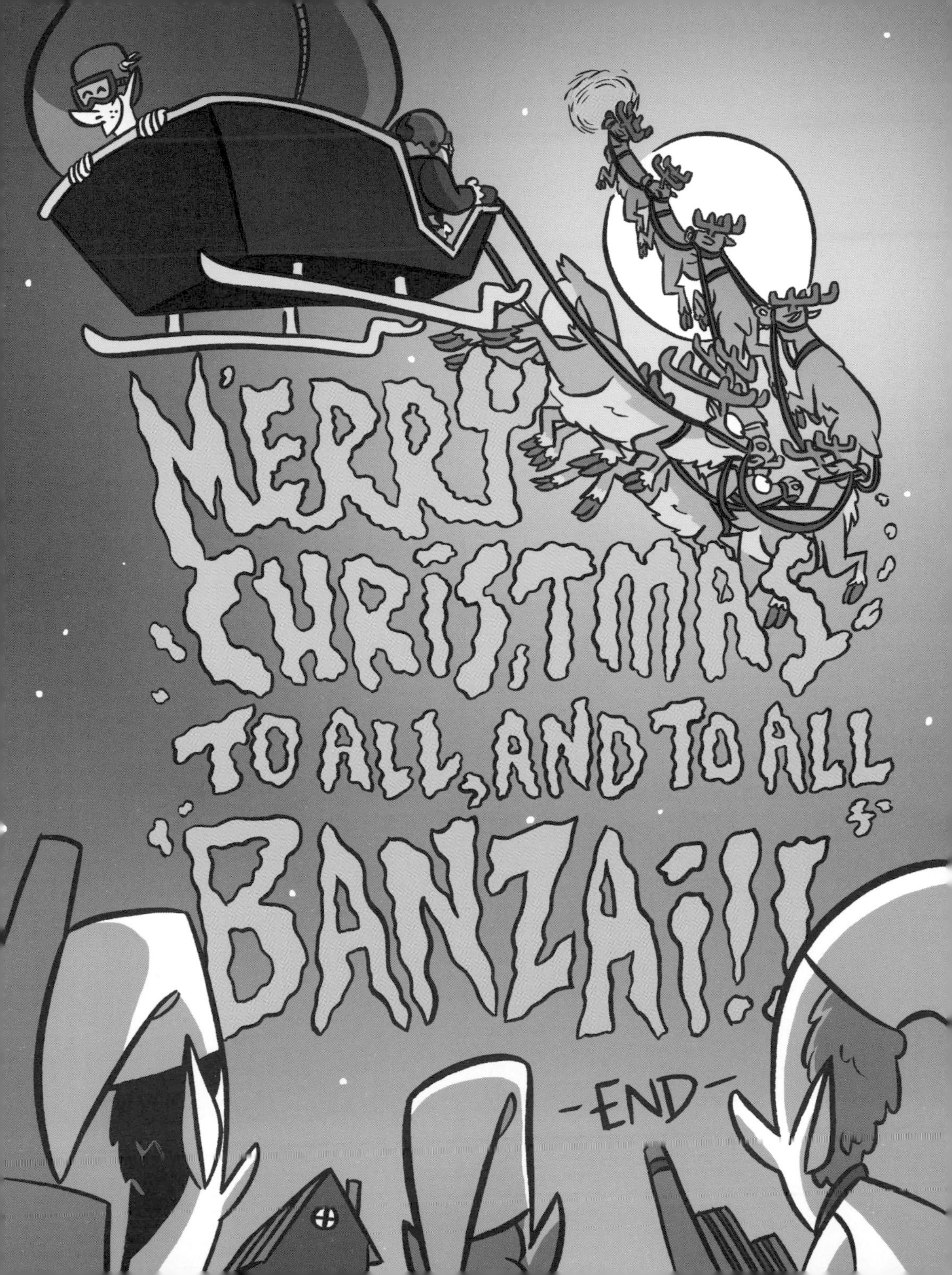
MERRY CHRISTMAS
TO ALL, AND TO ALL
BANZAI!!
-END-

Nathaniel Marunas grew up in New York City when there was more artwork on the subway cars than in all Gotham's museums combined. He contributed to the rise of videogame culture by feeding his collection of silver Kennedy half dollars into the change machines at the local arcade, and did his part to keep the comic book stores in his neighborhood alive by buying nearly everything, no matter how crappy. By watching kung fu films and reading such comics masterpieces as *The Adventures of Luther Arkwright* and *Lone Wolf and Cub* throughout college, he managed to arm himself with almost no professionally applicable skills whatsoever. Today, Nathaniel is grateful to be gainfully employed as a book editor in New York, despite the city's efforts to have all the city's "undesirables" shipped to sea on a trash barge.

This book never would have been possible without the encouragement and creative efforts of an incredible team of smart, enthusiastic people. I bow my head in respect to Erik Craddock, whose particular style of *bujitsu*, armed with brush and pixel, is unquestionable; he brought the characters in this work to life with great skill and humor, and his coinage of the title for this installment of Santa's manga adventures was particularly inspired. Second, I'd like to humbly say *domo arigato* to my truly excellent editors at Razorbill, Kristen Pettit and Eloise Flood, whose thoughtful and constructive comments on the work at every stage not only prevented me from looking foolish, they made the story better in every way. Third, I gratefully lay out an offering of rice, sake, water, salt, and evergreen branches on the *ozen* in honor of the gods and goddesses at Quirk Packaging: Lynne Yeamans, for her careful design oversight and work on the cover; Marion Vitus and John Green, for their coloring efforts; Marion again for lettering; and, last but certainly not least, *sensei* Sharyn Rosart, whose sage counsel and never-flagging encouragement made this entire process an absolute joy.

Erik Craddock grew up in Babylon, New York, during the 1980s and '90s on a steady diet of comics, video games, and pop culture. He graduated from New York City's prestigious School of Visual Arts (SVA), where he produced the underground comics *Stone Rabbit*, *Craddock!*, and *The Justice Seven*, and received honors and awards including the Rhodes Family Award for Excellence in Cartooning. Erik worked on the animated series *The Venture Brothers* and *SKWOD*, as well as the movie *Duplex*. Currently, Erik works as a director for online animations, a consultant, and as a character designer and storyboard artist. Erik's work can also be found in the permanent collection of the Museum of Comic and Cartooning Art (MOCCA) in New York.

Erik would like to thank his mom and dad, his brother Chris, and Oma for their unending support and belief in his future success. He would also like to thank Renshi Allie Alberigo of the Hanata Dojo in West Islip and his friends in the L.I. Ninjutsu Centers for all the good years of training, as well as providing inspiration for this work; Raina Telgemeier for recommending him for this job; the crew at Quirk Packaging; the good folks at Cosmic Comics in New York; and his friends and teachers at SVA.

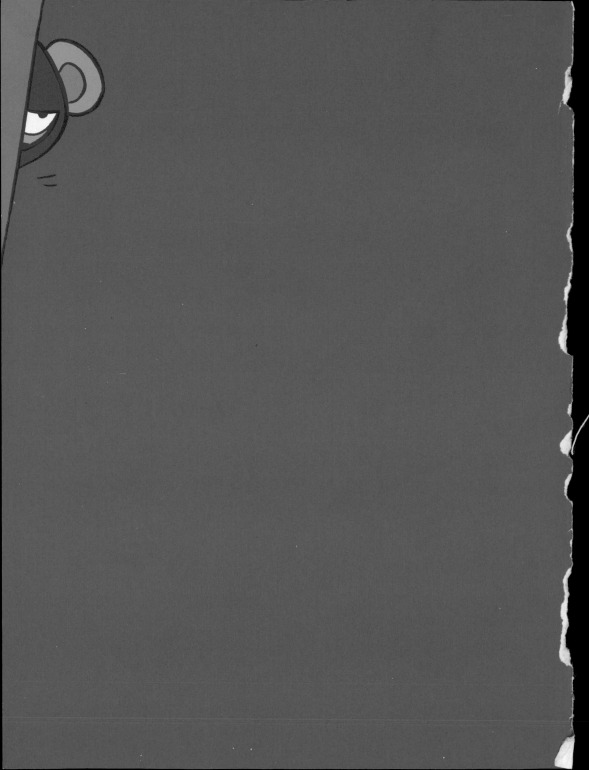